NEXT

YEAR,

FOR

SURE

NEXT YEAR,

FOR SURE

Zoey Leigh Peterson

DOUBLEDAY CANADA

Doubleday Canada and colophon are registered trademarks of Penguin Random House Canada Limited

Library and Archives Canada Cataloguing in Publication

Peterson, Zoey Leigh, author
      Next year, for sure / Zoey Leigh Peterson.

Issued in print and electronic formats.
ISBN 978-0-385-68677-8 (paperback).--ISBN 978-0-385-68675-4 (epub)

      I. Title.

PS8623.E4743N49 2017   C813'.6   C2016-902972-7
                                               C2016-902973-5

Cover design: Jaya Miceli
Cover art: "Unnamed Affection" © Jarek Puczel
Cover lettering: Grace Han
Printed and bound in the USA

Published in Canada by Doubleday Canada,
a division of Penguin Random House Canada Limited

www.penguinrandomhouse.ca

10 9 8 7 6 5 4 3 2

Penguin
Random House
DOUBLEDAY CANADA

For Susannah

Signals At Sea
Annie Dillard

—Charles H. Cugle, *Cugle's Practical Navigation*, 1936.

(*If the flags in A's hoist cannot be made out, B keeps her answering pennant at the "Dip" and hoists the signal "OWL" or "WCX."*)

CXL   Do not abandon me.

A   I am undergoing a speed trial.

D   Keep clear of me—I am maneuvering
             with difficulty.

F   I am disabled. Communicate with me.

G   I require a pilot.

P   Your lights are out, or burning badly.

U   You are standing into danger.

X   Stop carrying out your intentions.

K   You should stop your vessel instantly.

L   You should stop. I have something
             important to communicate.

R   You may feel your way past me.

SEPTEMBER

CHAPTER 1

Next Year, For Sure

If you put the religion books on one shelf, it makes god look like a phase you went through. Like a deck you were going to build until you got a few manuals and all the tools and then didn't. No, it's better to have those books scattered seemingly at random, snuggled between a history of space travel and a slim volume of found poems. Then it's clear that spirituality is just one facet in a richly lived life. It says you are open to possibilities.

Chris doesn't even know if Emily believes in god. (Or poetry, for that matter, or interplanetary travel.) He knows that she swears impressively but never goddamns anything—not once in their seven conversations. He knows that she lives in a crowded, bustling house called Ahimsa, but the house would have been named long before Emily moved to town and took over this part of his brain. And he knows that when he asked if she'd like to come apartment-sit over the long weekend, she used the word *sanctuary*, and said it in a way that stilled the air.

I think I have a crush on Emily, he tells Kathryn in the shower. This is where they confide crushes.

A heart crush or a boner crush? Kathryn says.

He doesn't know how to choose. It's not particularly sexual, his crush. He hasn't thought about Emily that way. And Chris would never say boner. But it's not just his heart, either. It's his molecules.

So he tells Kathryn about his molecules. How the first time he met Emily, it felt like his DNA had been re-sequenced. How he felt an instant kinship and a tenderness that was somehow painful. How, whenever he talks to her, he comes away feeling hollowed out and nauseous like after swimming too long in a chlorinated pool. And how—this, sheepishly—he has spent days arranging and rearranging their bookshelves and postcards and takeout menus, to make the apartment not only as welcoming as possible but as informative. As compelling.

You're awesome, Kathryn says.

Kathryn gets into bed still wet, the way she likes, and Chris makes the bed around her. A pillow between her thighs, a kiss on each knee, one arm tucked between the sheet and the blanket. She does this thing, this purring sound in her throat, which he has never been able to approximate.

Chris slides under the covers and wraps himself around her. She burrows, nestles with contentment, but then seems sad.

I wish Sharon and Kyle were coming, she says.

Me too, he says. But it'll still be good. He holds her and tells her all the ways it will still be good. Four days in the woods— no cars, no phones, no people. Four days alone with her favourite person in her favourite place with her favourite foods. She smiles. He walks her through each meal they've planned, the ingredients premeasured and packed into satisfyingly compact little bundles on the backs of their bikes. She nods and mmms until she starts to twitch and is away.

Chris tries to let himself be pulled down by the warm suck of her undertow, but he is left lying in the dark. In his head, he starts to compose the offhand note he will write as they rush off the next morning. Hi Emily, Please make yourself at home. There is white wine in the fridge, and red—Hi Emily, Everything you see is yours. Hi Emily, I love you. Hi Emily, We'll be back Monday night. Hope you have a great weekend! Love, Chris.

Love, Chris & Kathryn.

Kathryn & Chris.

It's a two-hour ride to the big ferry, then another two hours on the other side, then a smaller ferry, another ride. By the time they get to the campsite, it will be dusk. But right now it's still dewy and cool and they are taking it easy. Normally, there'd be the four of them riding in a line, and he knows Kathryn's favourite thing is to ride at the back and watch them all snaking through the city, loaded with gear. Today they are riding side by side because it is too lonely not to.

Kathryn has been a little sad all morning, so to cheer her up, Chris has been amusing her with the fussy, imperceptible measures he has taken to prepare the apartment for Emily: vacuuming the coils behind the fridge, relabelling their ragtag spice jars, hiding their exercise tapes. Nothing invigorates Kathryn like a good crush—more often hers, but especially his—and she was quick to make it into a game they could both play. After they'd put on fresh sheets for Emily, Kathryn insisted they roll around on the just-made bed.

If it looks too neat, she said, it feels forbidding. What you want is a deep, deep sense of clean, yes, but then a surface that is—

(And here she made a gesture that was at once inviting and nonchalant.)

They rolled and cavorted on the bed until it needed to be made all over again.

On the smaller ferry, they stand away from their bicycles so they don't have to field questions from bored drivers. They lean on the railing and gaze out over the water.

I used to always see whales on the ferry when I was a kid, Kathryn says. She is stretching her calf muscle without taking her eyes off the horizon. I thought that was the whole point, she says, the whales. The first time they didn't come, I told my mom she should get our money back.

Chris always likes this story. He likes to look inside her brain and see how it works, like an ant farm or a cutaway model of a submarine—he never gets tired of looking.

He tells her, again, about the time his family went camping and how he woke up one morning to find two killer whales playing in the water just off the shore, and how he stood there for half an hour, not twenty feet from his family asleep in their tents, and never woke them up.

Her eyes well with fresh love. Sometimes Chris wonders if Kathryn remembers his stories; it often seems like she's hearing them for the first time. But then at other times they'll be talking and Kathryn will pluck a thread from a story Chris himself has long since forgotten, and he feels profoundly plumbed.

I hope you'd wake me up, she says.

I would definitely wake you up, he says.

He doesn't know why he hadn't woken his family. Or why he had hoped, almost prayed, that they wouldn't wake up on their own. Or why, after only a few minutes, Chris had started to wish the whales would leave, even while he couldn't stop staring and gasping with joy.

Kathryn presses into him, and they stare out over the teeming ocean. They see no whales.

Setting up the tent is awkward. Chris gets agitated by small objects when he is tired and sticky. Usually, Kathryn does the tents with Kyle while Sharon and Chris make dinner. They have a whole system.

Tonight the tent seems needlessly complex. Kathryn, though, is a good teacher. She talks him through each pole and peg as if she were talking him down from a very wide ledge. He likes learning things from her. He has a list in his head: how to develop film in the bathtub, how to can tomatoes, how to spell his name in sign language. By the time the tent is up, it is past dark and they are too tired to cook. They sit in the tent and eat a jar of peanut butter.

Kathryn falls asleep in her clothes, mid-sentence. Chris rummages through her backpack in the dark and finds her mouthguard. He holds it up to her lips and whispers in her ear. Baby bird, he says. She opens her jaw and feels for the plastic guard with her lips. He watches her pull it into her mouth and hears it snap into place.

Chris lies back and listens to the tide coming in or going out. He wants to stay in this moment, this ache of contentedness, but his mind is already starting to skip and skitter. He tries to tunnel down into his body, to feel the way his muscles are singing from the ride, the way his cells are feasting on the fat and protein of the peanut butter, the way his bones know that they are resting on the earth. But he thinks: Emily.

Emily.

Emily.

Emily.

Kathryn calls it the Tuna Voice. On their fifth anniversary, after nearly a lifetime without meat, Kathryn woke up in the night to a voice in her head. The voice said TunaTunaTunaTunaTuna. She couldn't sleep. She couldn't read. She couldn't eat. Or she could eat, but it didn't make any difference. For weeks she tried fatty omega acids and vitamin B, but all she could think was TunaTunaTunaTunaTuna. Finally, she gave up and ate a damn tuna fish sandwich and the voice stopped. She almost cried for two days. About a year later, the voice came back, and she immediately ate a tuna fish sandwich. Now she buys one can of tuna a year and keeps it in the cupboard and doesn't call herself a vegetarian.

Maybe you just need to eat Emily, she says over breakfast.

Chris makes a face.

Once a year, she says.

He'd like to change the subject, but he can't think of anything else.

Without Sharon and Kyle, the day feels long.

———

Without Sharon and Kyle, they eat lunch too early, and then dinner too early. And then the sun won't go down.

Years ago, before Sharon and Kyle, they had come here with other friends. Dori and Brett the first time, but Dori and Brett seemed to believe that the point of camping together was so the men and the women could get away from each other. Dori kept saying things like, Why don't you boys go explore while we get dinner organized. And later, to Kathryn, conspiratorially, Why don't we make the menfolk wash the dishes.

Michael and Pat had come another year, but what made Michael and Pat such sparkling dinner guests made them exhausting campers. They were funny, inquisitive, and perpetually on, quickly filling each silence with witty banter and innuendo until after three days it felt like the most important thing in the world was for four people to be able to sit in the woods and not talk.

Then there was Susan and Mark, whose irony and just-kidding insults gradually became toxic. And Jamie and Rhen, who were fine, but who never stopped feeling like company.

Really, Sharon and Kyle were perfect. Sharon and Kyle took turns telling stories. Sharon and Kyle asked questions and listened to your answers. Even when you paused to take a breath, even when you circled back to find the words you hadn't found before, they didn't interrupt. Sharon and Kyle got tipsy from the same number of drinks. Sharon and Kyle never said, Too bad— it's three against one. Sharon and Kyle went to bed at the right time and didn't sleep all day and make you tiptoe around the campsite. Sharon and Kyle pulled different stories out of Kathryn—stories Chris had never heard before.

The only problem with Sharon and Kyle is the question too important to ask: Will they come next year?

They go to bed before dark, and wait in each other's arms for sleep.

I hope you don't leave me for Emily, Kathryn says.

I'm not going to leave you for Emily, he says.

He doesn't want to leave her for Emily. He wants to be smart, to be a grown-up, to learn from his mistakes. Besides, it wouldn't work.

Chris knows, just from their few conversations, that Emily's days are bursting with potlucks and benefits and this friend's opening and that friend's closing, and he knows how this would go. For a couple of weeks, it would be extraordinary. He would rise to every occasion. He would be fun and vibrant, full of fresh stories and observations. Her friends would love him. Because he can be impressive; that's what everyone says. But after a while, Chris would reach the bottom of his reserves. He would need a night to recharge. He would need *most* nights to recharge. Emily would stay home to be with him, or she'd go without him and be sad about his absence, but either way, her friends would take it personally. And when Chris says that he needs to recharge, they'd say, Exactly, all the more reason to come out. They'd say it'll be just what he needs. Because they can't understand that the thing that rejuvenates them is the thing that drains Chris. That going out and having fun is harder than work.

And then Emily, after months of feeling isolated and losing touch with who she is, finally breaks up with him. Or she should. And everyone is miserable. Him, Emily, Kathryn. Kathryn who had been the perfect fit all along.

While the tent fills with their exhaled breath, Chris plays the scenario out in his head like a film reel, watching the relationships implode in real time, then watching in reverse, trying to inoculate himself against the voice whispering at the edges of his brain.

When he wakes up, Kathryn is gone. There is a note on the picnic table, waiting under a rock. She has seen people in kayaks and has gone to find out the rental rates. She loves him. And under this, she has drawn a picture of him sleeping, all furrowed and earnest.

He cooks breakfast like a ceremony, channelling all his errant feelings of tenderness into her food. She is Kathryn the Amazing. His favourite person in the world. He tries to prolong the preparation, to tease the food along, so that when she returns, everything will be moments from ready, like magic. But then suddenly it is done, and Kathryn is still gone.

He putters around the campsite, tidying their gear, folding the discarded clothes that have accumulated at the foot of their sleeping pads. He oils her chain. He adjusts his brakes. After a while, he eats breakfast alone, and sets Kathryn's aside for her.

Chris reads her letter again. He stares into the loops of her g's, the cavities in her vowels, and senses he has said too much. It is time to stop talking about Emily. But he doesn't know how to not share everything with Kathryn. He doesn't know how to keep a secret from her. Or how to just shrug and smile when she asks what he's thinking, which is what she asks when she comes back. She is wearing a life jacket.

———

The kayak is a two-person deal, and big. It was the last they had. Cinched into the rear cockpit, he feels he is part of a two-headed sea monster—half human, half boat, half human.

They negotiate their way along the shore, too nervous for the open water where the current sometimes takes people away.

For years, Sharon and Kyle have been trying to hike round to the other side of the island, seemingly impossible to reach by land. This, Chris knows, is where the kayak is headed. They will see the other side of the island, he and Kathryn, and they will tell Sharon and Kyle, and Sharon and Kyle will say they can't believe they missed it, and next year for sure.

Chris watches Kathryn's steady strokes and eases his rhythm to complement hers. He tries to stroke left when she strokes right, right when she strokes left. He thinks one of them is supposed to be steering, but they seem to be finding a course together, pushing wordlessly toward the far point of the shore, and then the next point, and then the point beyond that.

Do you want to kiss her? Kathryn says.

Chris didn't even know he was thinking about Emily.

From the rear of the kayak, he can't see Kathryn's face, only her back, her hair, her elbows. He studies the back of her head, trying to read her. She is leaning into her strokes, getting tired.

I don't want to kiss her, he says.

He doesn't want to kiss her. He wants what comes after. After the kissing and the undressing and the confiding. After the discovery and the familiarity and the gradual absence of kissing. He wants the intimacy of friends who used to be lovers.

They paddle around an outcropping in silence.

Because if you want to kiss her, she says, tell me and we can have that conversation.

Okay, he says.

Across the back of her life jacket is stencilled the word MEDIUM. He thinks: Medium. Seer. Soothsayer.

They turn back, unsure how far they've gone. They take turns paddling, and sometimes let themselves float along.

Sleep World

Forty-seven minutes is a long time to kill in a mattress store when you don't need a mattress. For the first couple of laps, the salespeople kindly ignore Kathryn. She has explained that she is waiting for someone. It's early on a Tuesday morning, and the salespeople are still handing each other cups of coffee and debriefing on last night's television.

Kathryn wanders the store, trying to look purposeful. She studies each mattress in turn. She contemplates their regal names. She peers into a small cutaway section of mattress with its isolated springs pressed up against Plexiglas. They look battered and desperate, like the animals in the brochures that keep coming in the mail.

Eventually, one of the young salesmen is sent over to check on her. Kathryn affirms, again, that she is waiting for a friend, that it is the friend who needs a mattress, and that she herself is entirely content with her current mattress, though this is not strictly true. Her own bed is sagging and problematic, but Chris likes it.

The young salesman returns to the pack with this information. They keep talking amongst themselves about this show and that show, but Kathryn can feel them watching her with suspicion. She tries to imagine what they might suspect. That she is going to sneak out of the store with a queen-size box spring in her bag? That she is going to slit the long, soft belly of a mattress and hide evidence inside? That she is going to move into their showroom with several temperamental cats and set up camp? What is their worst-case scenario?

Now that Sharon owns a car, she is late to everything. The car was part of a story that began with Sharon not having a baby and ended with her and Kyle moving to a condo with cream carpets.

On paper, their new place is not even that far away. A forty-minute ride from Chris and Kathryn's—thirty if you really pedal. Kathryn and Sharon had routinely cycled twice that distance when they were in grad school together, but the miles feel somehow longer in this new direction. Bike paths end unceremoniously, spitting you out onto noisy highways. The cars move faster and seem angrier.

Back when Sharon and Kyle lived across the alley, the four of them would see each other almost every day. Sometimes to borrow a lemon or envelope or screwdriver, other times because the news was too terrible to watch alone.

Now though, they don't show up at each other's back door with a bottle of wine or a birthday cake. They don't phone each other and say, We made too much pasta, do you guys want to come eat with us? Instead they say, What does week after next look like? They say, Can we do it at *our* place? They say, Hey I'm coming into town to look at mattresses, why don't you come along and we can catch up.

When Sharon arrives, much is forgiven. The salespeople are not suspicious of Sharon. They are charmed and intrigued by her princess-vs-pea dilemma—a series of fine beds that all felt perfect for the first hour, but then this nagging ache would creep up her leg and into her spine. It's fun to watch Sharon do her thing. She is getting everyone on board, like they are her students. Kathryn feels lucky to be here playing hooky with Sharon on a Tuesday morning while her work sits at home on the desk.

Here is what I propose, says Sharon to the gathered sales force. You guys pretend I'm not here and let me lie around in your beds all day like a weirdo. Then at the end of the day, I hand you my credit card and show you the bed you just sold me.

This amuses the salespeople and they bring out paper booties and special pillows for different kinds of sleepers—side sleepers, stomach sleepers—and a secret notebook with all the pricing information and talking points. Thus equipped, Sharon and Kathryn are set adrift in the sea of mattresses.

Now, says Sharon once they are alone, let's get in bed and then I want to hear all about this Emily thing.

Kathryn had told Sharon about the Emily thing during an inadvertent phone call inspired by Neanderthals. She'd been on the couch watching a BBC program on Neanderthals, the last of a people, and she had suddenly felt so much love for Sharon, and so much longing, that she picked up the phone and dialed her number without thinking.

Sharon was half watching the same show and paying some bills, and they talked about work for a while and how it must feel for an actor to be cast as a Neanderthal.

Then Sharon had asked what was up, and asked in such a way that Kathryn felt that something should be up. And so, to have something to say, Kathryn told her that Chris had a crush on some Emily he sees at the laundromat—which is fine, people get crushes—but that he had invited this person to stay in their apartment while they were away for the long weekend, to house-sit, to sleep in their bed, and that that felt weird. This got Sharon's interest. They talked about it hotly for several minutes—Sharon being emphatic and scandalized in gratifying ways—until Sharon was so sorry, but she had to head down to a condo meeting.

Now Sharon is going to want the whole story. Everything is a story now with Sharon. But Kathryn isn't sure what else to say. Chris hasn't mentioned Emily since that weekend. After bringing her up constantly in the weeks leading up to her stay, now he can't even be drawn into conversation about her. When Kathryn asks what Emily looks like or what colour her hair is, Chris can't say. All that Kathryn knows about Emily is what she left behind in their apartment: in the bathroom, a tin of lip balm with a sliding lid that is satisfying to open and close; in the recycling, an unrinsed jar of some paste that makes the whole apartment smell velvety; in the bedroom, nothing, although both their clock radios were unplugged; and on the refrigerator, a three-page letter of thanks, politely addressed to both of them, but clearly written for Chris and filled with such candour and fellow-ship that it felt too intimate to read. Kathryn had read it twice.

All this she has already told Sharon on the phone while the Neanderthals failed to adapt.

Kathryn considers now telling Sharon about the misspellings in the letter, not just Kathryn's name, but in nearly every line. But she cannot think of a way to say this without sounding petty. Finally, she resolves to say this: There is no story. There are just these feelings that come and go. Feelings without a beginning, middle, and end.

But by the time they are settled into a bed, they are already talking about sex.

Since buying the condo, Sharon and Kyle have been out of sync, sexually. Morning has always been their time. Morning and night for the first couple years, but mornings in particular. These days, though, Kyle's brain wakes up making lists and doesn't remember it has a body until it's time to leave for work. Now Sharon has found a solution: oats. Apparently, a quarter cup of steel-cut oats right before bed has Kyle waking up like his former self.

That's why I was late getting here, Sharon says. She doesn't actually wink.

Kathryn rolls onto her side and stares out over the empty mattresses. They're like ice floes. Can you steer an ice floe? Or do you just go where it takes you?

How did you figure that out? Kathryn asks. The oat thing.

Ann-Marie, from our building, she told me about it, says Sharon.

Kathryn has met this Ann-Marie once, at Sharon and Kyle's housewarming. Ann-Marie was in the kitchen blending margaritas and warming tortillas in a cast-iron pan she'd brought from her place across the hall. Let me take that, said Ann-Marie, plucking a dirty plate from Kathryn's hand. This kitchen is exactly like mine, so I already know my way around, said Ann-Marie, though Kathryn could see the sink right there.

You should try it, says Sharon of the oats. This, Kathryn understands, is a reference to Chris, and Kathryn feels a vague urge to defend him.

Chris has what Kathryn calls a high cuddle drive. He kisses her awake every morning, he reaches out to stroke her arm while they read the paper, he hugs her for whole minutes, which she loves. And okay, so they don't have a lot of sex. But when they do—usually on a Sunday, sometimes when the air turns crisp—it can sprawl across the whole afternoon and into the evening, luxurious and playful and sweet.

This isn't working for me, says Sharon, rising from the bed. Too mooshy, she says.

They drift through the beds, Sharon pressing her palm firmly down into each mattress and holding it there, eyes closed, as if communing with the bed's essential nature. Kathryn looks at price tags. Some of the beds are so unaccountably expensive that Kathryn—if it was up to her—wouldn't even pause in front of them, wouldn't give them the satisfaction.

Sharon is lingering near a four-thousand-dollar bed. She has slid her hand under the foam pad and is palpating the springs, dispassionately, like a doctor. She is in fact a middle school teacher.

Didn't they just buy a bed, Sharon and Kyle? (Kathryn remembers precisely: it was an engagement present to themselves.) Did they sell that bed? Where does four thousand dollars come from? How do you buy a condo, and then a bed, and then another bed?

There was a time when Kathryn might have asked Sharon these questions. Actually, there was a time she wouldn't have had to ask—the answers would have bubbled to the surface while they helped each other put away groceries or stood in line together to cash their student loans. When they were part of the slow unspooling of each other's lives.

Sharon has sunk herself into the four-thousand-dollar mattress. Kathryn is converting the price in her head. Four thousand dollars is her food for an entire year. It is the dental work Chris needs. It is x hours of copy-editing plus y hours of indexing, over the ten-year life of the bed, for a total of z hours per year. Kathryn climbs onto the exquisite bed.

Sharon holds Kathryn's hand as they lie staring up at the acoustic panels.

This is the one, Sharon says. Her hand feels softer than it used to, and bigger, in a four-thousand-dollar bed.

Sharon used to be cheap. When they were students, when money was a thing, Sharon was flamboyantly frugal, a loud champion of all things scrounged or redeemed.

One time, Sharon and Kyle had shown up at their door late one evening, exultant, because the video store was throwing out old VHS tapes. Sharon had rescued *The Great Muppet Caper* from a cardboard box on the sidewalk, just as the rain was starting to fall.

Chris pulled the futon off the frame and onto the living room floor, and the four of them sardined themselves under two overlapping blankets and watched and cheered and made smart and dumb jokes, until Kathryn thought she might hyperventilate from laughing.

Later, exhausted by their own hilarity, they watched in silence, a blissful stupor washing over their bodies. Kathryn loved these people, loved living on this futon island with them, and it was at this moment—as the movie rounded into the third act—that she began to think about the four of them falling asleep here in front of the TV, and the four of them waking up in the morning and making breakfast together and deciding what to do with their Sunday, the four of them. Kyle was already drifting off, soughing faintly between songs. Soon Chris was asleep, too, furrowing and scrunching his sincere face. Finally, it was just Sharon and Kathryn holding hands and fading in and out as the tireless puppets saved the day. Then the credits were rolling and Sharon was squeezing her hand, then letting it go. She was reaching for Kyle's shoulder, rubbing him slowly awake.

You guys can stay, Kathryn had said. You should stay.

Sharon smiled, and kept rousing Kyle, who made a low, assenting rumble.

You should stay, Kathryn said again. It felt strangely urgent.

But now Kyle was standing, his eyes still closed, and Sharon was leading him to the door.

Thank you for a perfect night, Sharon said.

Kathryn locked the door behind them and stood there trying to reabsorb her feelings. She could hear Chris stirring in the other room. He was calling out to her—making an endearing joke that had threaded through the evening—and she was inexplicably irritated and hot and a kind of angry that she could not name. She did not answer. She washed the dishes loudly and wrestled the futon back onto the frame and did not go to bed until Chris was surely asleep. By the next day, Sharon and Kyle were engaged.

———

This, ladies, is as good as it gets. So says the salesman. The reigning king of beds, he says. He begins to enumerate the many features of this noble mattress. Kathryn can see the contents of his nostrils.

They have only been in this bed for twenty minutes, so Kathryn waits for Sharon to drive the salesman away, remind him of their deal. But Sharon does not drive him away. She encourages him. She calls him Gary, which is his name. She asks Gary how long the warranty is, she asks about coil count. They talk admiringly to each other about the bed while Kathryn stares into a halogen light. She is thinking again about that letter, magneted to her fridge.

And what do you think? the salesman asks Kathryn. Kathryn doesn't understand the question.

She's just keeping me company, Sharon says, letting go of Kathryn's hand. Sharon explains to the salesman that her boyfriend—fiancé actually—can sleep on anything and so bed-shopping with him is impossible because he dozes off on every bed they try.

The salesman makes a half-neutered observation about men and women and Sharon laughs. Sharon and the salesman begin to rehearse the differences between men and women.

But Chris would be here. If Kathryn had a pain in her leg, if Kathryn was unable to sleep at night, Chris would be here beside her, even if he was bored. But he wouldn't be bored. He would be engaged. He would turn it into a game. He would make up a backstory for each mattress. He would tell her about their childhoods as beanbags, imbuing each bed with hopes and ambitions and tragic flaws that he and Kathryn might recognize and grow to love. And Kathryn would mostly listen, but would occasionally blurt out some bit of business that he would seamlessly integrate into the story.

And when the time came to decide, Chris would listen to Kathryn's messy, rambling anxieties about where the bed was made, what the factory conditions were for the workers, and did she really need a new bed at all, and didn't most of the world sleep on mats not nearly as comfortable as the bed they already had. And when she got overwhelmed by the morality of it and all the choices and the expense and the materialism and she started to panic, he would put his arm around her and guide her out of the store and across the street to the noodle place and he would get a bowl of food in front of her. He would sit beside her in the vinyl booth and surround her with his quiet goodness, soak up all her terror and despair and absorb it like a charcoal filter, until she felt worthy of love and a non-debilitating bed and could march herself back across the street and buy a decent mattress. And when some salesman told them that men are like this and women are like that, Kathryn would know that she and Chris were on the same side and that Gary was on the other. Because Kathryn and Chris are a team.

Sharon is sitting up now, digging through her bag. She is buying the four-thousand-dollar bed. Kathryn wonders at the quiet snap of this decision. How one minute Sharon did not know, and then the next minute she did. It is only eleven thirty in the morning.

Kathryn has not said any of the things she meant to say. She meant to say that, yes, the thought of Emily eats at her. That she feels colonized by that letter, planted like a flag in her kitchen. That sometimes when Kathryn comes home and the letter has been moved slightly, she wishes that Emily would disappear and have never existed, but that sometimes she wishes it was Chris who would disappear, or she herself, or that nobody had ever existed and the planet was still choked with algae and God was pleased. Other times, she hears some dumb song on the radio that makes her feel connected to everything—mattress salesmen and earwigs and crying babies—and she wants Chris to do whatever he needs to do to be happy. If he needs to kiss Emily, then kiss her. Or worse even. She just wants him to be happy. She wants him to be happy so he can make *her* happy.

Sometime this week would be ideal, says Sharon.

Sharon has her day-planner out, making arrangements for the mattress to be delivered. Kathryn lets her eyes skim through Sharon's week, the appointments and the half-familiar names. It's mostly wedding stuff. Then she sees her own name:

Sleep World

(w/Kathryn!)

Next to her name is drawn a small heart. The whole day is blocked off. Kathryn wonders if they will now have lunch and sit on some heated patio drinking bellinis and talking about big and small things, or if the unexpected efficiency of this purchase will inspire Sharon to see how many other tasks she can squeeze into her so-called sick day.

Kathryn doesn't mind either way. She is ready to go home. She has something to say to Chris. It is starting to take up space in her mouth. She wants him to be happy. What is her worst-case scenario?

CHAPTER 3

Weekend Projectionist

Chris has never asked someone out on a date before. On the last day of junior high, when it had become clear that he would never ask her, Cynthia Welland had asked Chris to see *Ghostbusters* with her, and he had been happy to go. He liked movies and he liked watching them with people, and when they emerged from the theatre into the blinding day, he could suddenly think of a whole list of movies they should see together.

They saw one matinee a week for the entire summer and when school started again in the fall, Chris and Cynthia were generally considered boyfriend-girlfriend, which was how things stood until the following spring, when Chris accidentally fell in love with Cynthia's best friend, Robyn Joffe, who had come along on most of their dates and who argued good-naturedly with Chris about everything. Chris enjoyed arguing with Robyn. He liked it when she said, That's a very good point, and then went on to make an even better point of her own, and he liked the feeling of his mind being changed. Chris would phone Cynthia every night and, more often than not, Robyn would be there, sitting beside her on the bed, offering comments, little provocations, until Cynthia handed over the receiver and the two of them, Chris and Robyn, would talk until it was time to hang up.

Chris did nothing about these feelings for Robyn, of course. It's possible it never occurred to him that he might do something. But then, while Chris was crying at his grandmother's funeral in Prince George, Robyn and Cynthia had a long talk, and when he got back to school he found he was now boyfriend-girlfriend with Robyn, and it was Cynthia Welland who gamely tagged along on their agreeably chaste dates.

Chris and Robyn had decided to wait until they were married— or at least until university, which they applied to together, editing each other's admissions essays in Cynthia Welland's basement— not because of any religious compunction, but because sex, along with alcohol, had made their classmates into insufferable idiots whose only form of conversation was recounting, in fantastic detail, the drunken escapades they professed to barely remember. That's what Robyn said anyway, and that seemed right to Chris. He didn't much like anyone at school, except Robyn and Cynthia. And so, to distance themselves from such barbarism, Chris and Robyn and Cynthia Welland spent their Friday nights reading to each other from course catalogues and designing elaborate flowcharts of which classes they would all take together and which they would take separately and then teach to each other.

On long weekends, they went on campus visits, which is how Chris met Celeste, a twenty-two-year-old French Lit major at the University of British Columbia who smelled like spice drops and had interesting things to say about everything. (Robyn was touring Reed that weekend, because it was decision time and they were being strategic—travelling separately, then coming home with detailed reports.)

Celeste was a student ambassador in charge of the Student Life portion of the tour and, as the afternoon progressed, seemed to be directing her comments to Chris alone. Later that night, while Chris slept in a guest dorm with three drunk football players, Celeste somehow put an orange on his pillow with the word *Want?* inscribed on the rind in ballpoint pen.

Chris did not sleep with Celeste, not then, but what he did do was not go home. What he did do was move into Celeste's off-campus apartment with her bowing bookshelves and her despised roommate, Rajika, and spend the rest of summer drinking plum wine from their neighbour's trees and reading Rimbaud and having long, circular arguments on the phone with Robyn in which he said there was no reason she shouldn't still come to Vancouver and take the classes they had planned together, that he *wanted* her to come, that he would help her find a place to live, and Robyn said, Have you been drinking? Are you drinking right now? Chris did not enjoy these arguments the way he had at home. And in September, Robyn went to Evergreen and Cynthia Welland sent Chris a letter saying he was an asshole.

Chris felt despicable and punished himself for months. Celeste said that (a) nobody should marry their high school puppyfriend, and (b) Chris had done the poor girl a favour if she didn't understand that, and that (c) guilt was a self-serving neurosis that was making him boring. Roommate Rajika said that (a) no one should marry anyone, because it is a system of ownership, and (b) Chris had done *himself* a favour, as we all do in life, and if Robyn was as smart as Chris claimed, then he should trust her to find her own happiness, and that (c) guilt, properly realized, could be the first step toward becoming a better person. Celeste and Rajika disagreed about everything, and more and more Chris found himself siding with Rajika. He wanted to be a better person and Rajika had a lot to say on the topic.

The year went badly for Celeste and when she finally moved out in a fury of broken dishes and academic suspension, she said that Chris was a slow poison and that he had betrayed her, that he and Rajika had formed an alliance against her, and that the two of them were clearly in love. Rajika said that the only poison was the psychopharmaceuticals that Celeste swallowed willingly and the vast quantities of plum wine she washed them down with, and that obviously Chris and Rajika were not in love but simply like-minded—two people who liked the dishes done and the compost taken out instead of rotting on the kitchen counter.

But once Celeste had blown out of their lives, it turned out they *were* in love. Ecstatically for some months, and then happily enough for almost a year, during which Rajika began to suspect that Chris was also in love with their Film Theory TA, Val, who was five years older than them and whose tutorials openly subverted Professor Stillman's brittle lecture notes with blistering counter-analysis from feminist film theory. Val frequently led a cadre of young disciples to underground screenings in downtown industrial buildings. Chris and Rajika were regulars. They watched unwatchable films of men eating human feces and South American cows being slaughtered in slow motion, and felt duly fortified against sentimentality and creeping hegemony. But Chris was not in love with Val. His crush on her was strictly academic. He didn't want to see her naked; he wanted to read her thesis and then read everything she cited in her thesis. And it is probably true that Val was not even aware of Chris's feelings until Rajika went on the attack.

Chris lived with Val for three years in graduate housing with an illegal cat named Cleo. Val taught Chris how to drink a single glass of wine in a way that made you feel smarter, not dumber. She took him to dinner parties with professors and deans where they engaged in long, rigorous debates about normativity. She played him Bessie Smith records, and Ethiopian jazz, and un-labelled cassettes that strangers sent her in the mail.

Val got Chris a job as the weekend projectionist at the local film society, where he spent the early nineties projecting the films of Laura Mulvey and trying not to fall in love with Penny, the volunteer coordinator, who every night after the last screen-ing took all the volunteers across the street for a drink, where she and Chris would deconstruct the movie as the volunteers tried to keep up, then faded and filtered out.

It was in this bar that Val had shown up to say in firm, even tones that she was done with this and that Chris should not come home, and in fact she would like his key. She said he might want to take a look at himself and this pattern of his. She said that part of being in love with someone is not falling in love with someone else.

Chris had cried there in the bar with Bonnie Raitt playing on the sound system because he still loved Val, and he still loved Rajika, and Robyn, and maybe even Celeste, because they had been his best friends and he didn't like anyone as much as he liked them, and because Cynthia Welland thought he was an ass-hole and probably still thought so. He cried because he could not figure out how to be a person who did not hurt people. And then he went home with Penny—because where else could he go at one in the morning?—but he did not sleep with her. He slept instead on her floor, refusing that first night even a pillow or blanket.

When he did finally crawl into Penny's bed—after six months of reflection and self-flagellation—Chris made a private vow that this was it, that his heart was closed, forsaking all others, forever amen. And for four years, it worked. For four years, he was absolutely mule-hearted in his devotion to Penny, despite growing evidence that they were not compatible outside of a darkened movie theatre or too-loud bar.

Penny could be combative and belittling and was frequently mean to people. She was prone to categorical statements that unnerved Chris, like, Sex is always about power, or, Your dad is never going to change.

Still, Chris was resolutely in love with her and was adored by her friends and was probably going to marry her when he met Kathryn. Kathryn the Amazing. Kathryn who was perfect in every way. Kathryn who he nobly ignored for a year. Kathryn who nine years later came home from mattress shopping and said, I want you to ask this Emily on a date.

————

PHONE CALL
SATURDAY 10:09 AM

CHRIS: May I please speak with Emily?

MAN: Hmm. A fine question. [*then, to the room*]
         Is Emily even here?

ROOM: I'm not sure she came home last night.
         Someone came in around two.
         Yeah, I heard the kettle.
         Was there bossa nova?

	[*The voices laugh. The man sighs into the phone.*]
MAN:	Hold on.
	[*The man is walking with the phone. The man is climbing stairs, maybe two or three, now stops.*]
MAN:	EMILY?
	[*There is an interval of silence. They all listen, Chris and the man and the voices in the room, together.*]
MAN:	We think she might be asleep.
CHRIS:	I can call back.
MAN:	Do you want to leave a message?
CHRIS:	[*He does not.*]

QUESTIONS

Is 2 a.m. a normal time for Emily to get home? Do they often hear her come in? Do they sleep with their doors open or closed in that house? Do they come down for breakfast dishevelled and pyjamaed? Is her mouth minty? If they thought she *hadn't* come home last night, where would they think she'd be? A boyfriend's? A girlfriend's? (Her letter gave no clues.) Or was she lonely? Was she staying out for one last song, one last drink, in case the person she was looking for—the person who would see her for who she is—was about to walk through the door? Was last night the night she finally found that person? Chris could have called yesterday. He could've called last week, when Kathryn first told him to. Instead, he spent the week sitting with the phone in his lap. Until Kathryn said, of her patience, Act now, supplies are limited.

PHONE CALL

SATURDAY 4:47 PM

CHRIS: Is Emily there?

WOMAN: She was.

[*In the background, people are singing. There is a piano, possibly a banjo.*]

WOMAN: I don't see her coat.

CHRIS: I can call back.

WOMAN: Sorry, is this Chris?

CHRIS: Uh. Yes.

WOMAN: Oh my god. How's it going?

CHRIS: It's going okay.

WOMAN: The shows are good?

CHRIS: Uh.

WOMAN: Where are you tonight?

CHRIS: I don't think I'm that Chris.

WOMAN: Who is this?

CHRIS: I'm a friend of Emily's. From this summer.

WOMAN: Oh, I thought you were Chris.

CHRIS: Maybe I'll call back.

QUESTIONS

How many people live in that house? Do they all use the one phone? How many times will that phone ring today? How many of those rings will be for Emily? How many will be someone calling to ask her out? Does everyone ask Emily out? Does she need one person in her life who doesn't ask her out? Chris could do that. He could be that person. Because why do this? Why put everyone through this? When was the last time Chris was up at 2 a.m.? This is what he tries to explain to Kathryn over dinner. Why do it at all? Why stand into danger? Why risk disaster when everything is fine as it is?

One date, Kathryn says. Then we'll talk.

————

PHONE CALL

SUNDAY 11:31 AM

CHILD: This is Himsa.

CHRIS: Hi there. Is Emily home?

CHILD: He wants Emily. [*this, to someone nearby*]

ADULT: [*indistinct*]

[*The child is being coached by someone. Chris wishes he had someone to coach him. He feels out-manned.*]

ADULT: Ask him if it's important.

CHILD: Are you important?

CHRIS: I can call back.

CHILD: We're having pancakes.

CHRIS: Pancakes, wow.

CHILD: Emily doesn't get any because she stayed up toooo late.

CHRIS: I'm sure she'll be sad.

CHILD: No, she's not sad. She's happy.

CHRIS: Why is she happy?

[*The child has already hung up the phone.*]

QUESTIONS

What makes Emily happy? Does the smell of pancakes filling her bedroom make her happy? Does living with all those people

35

make her happy? Does having children in her life make her happy? Do waterslides make her happy? Do sleeper cars on trains make her happy? Does she love the little fold-up sink? Does reading in bed when it's raining outside make her happy? Do small things make her happy, like a miniature Tokyo made of paper on a gymnasium floor? Or do big things make her happy, like a giant heart you can crawl right into and disappear? Does seeing him make her happy? Is he imagining it?

———

PHONE CALL

SUNDAY 5:35 PM

CHRIS: Is Emily there?

EMILY: Hey! I was just talking about you.

CHRIS: This is Chris.

EMILY: I know!

CHRIS: Chris Deming.

EMILY: I know, I know! I was just telling my house about you.

CHRIS: Really? What?

EMILY: That amazing dish rack you built.

CHRIS: Oh.

EMILY: We want to build one like it here.

[In fact, it was Kathryn who built the dish rack. She took a woodworking class to do it—knew exactly what she wanted to build and then went and learned enough to build it—and he will tell Emily this, but right now she is so glad to hear

36

from him and she is telling him about her weekend,
a weekend dominated by three best friends with
competing birthdays who can never agree on just
one thing to do. She ate three dinners in one day.
She saw a friend's new play and it made her angry
because of the way it portrayed schizophrenia and
she is still debating whether she should say
something to the friend about that. They talk
about the responsibility of the artist, and the best
food to eat on your birthday, and about little
things, things you don't talk about when you bump
into each other on the street because they feel too
small to pull out on a busy sidewalk where you
might get jostled. After an hour, one of her
housemates needs to use the phone.]

ANSWERS

There are six people living in the house. They might be looking for a seventh. Dim sum makes her happy. Thoughtful graffiti on billboards makes her happy. Everyone in fake moustaches makes her happy. 2 a.m. is somewhat later than usual. She would love to have dinner with him.

CHAPTER 4

Tandoori Oven

I have another rule, Kathryn says. She is sitting on their bed, watching Chris get ready. He is wearing his magic sweater, and no pants.

Kathryn says, Don't tell her things about me.

What things? Chris says. He is pacing. He can't decide which pants to wear.

I mean, don't *not* talk about me. I want to exist, she says. Just not private things.

I think that goes without saying, K.

It should all go without saying, Chris, but here we are.

She isn't being exactly fair, she knows, snapping at him like this. The date was Kathryn's idea. And she wasn't going to be this way. She was going to be cool and evolved, like a Joni Mitchell song. She was going to be magnanimous.

Chris sits down beside her on the bed. Of course you're going to exist, he says. He holds her. He says he loves her. Most of the time Kathryn knows that. He's her person. He's not going anywhere.

I can cancel, Chris says. And he could. It's still an hour before their date.

I don't want you to cancel, Kathryn says.

She has watched him planning for it all week. He has made notes in a little book that fits in his pocket. Things to talk about. Questions he might ask. Places they could go afterwards to just sit and talk. Kathryn has read these notes. They're sweet.

And Kathryn has her own plans. The house to herself and too much wine, a dumb movie, and a pint of strawberry ice cream. Chris is allergic to strawberries.

I'm just saying there are rules, Kathryn says. Rules have been dribbling out all week. Has Chris written those in his little book?

He is pulling on his grey pants when the doorbell rings. Why is the doorbell ringing?

I'm early, Emily says. Am I too early?

No, this is great, Chris assures her, though he is barely in his pants.

I'm terrible, Emily says. It's just I hate being late. She is beaming at Chris, and then at Kathryn, like a searchlight. You must be Kathryn, Emily says, and she steps in her sock feet across the room. Can I give you a hug? she says.

Of course, says Kathryn, unable to think of an alternative. They embrace like friends.

Kathryn wasn't going to be here for this. She was going to be at the video store picking out a movie too stupid for Chris. Now she is hugging this woman, her boyfriend's date. She's a nice hugger, though, Emily is. Solid and living and real. Kathryn can feel the heat rising from Emily's neck.

So you're coming to dinner with us? Emily says.

I can't, Kathryn says.

Oh no! says Emily. Why not? She looks genuinely disappointed.

I rented a movie, says Kathryn. A lie. That was one of the rules. No lying.

Oh please come, Emily says.

Kathryn doesn't know what to say. She looks to Chris for help. He has spent all week thinking up smart things to say.

You should come, Chris says. It'll be fun.

He's smiling. Emily is smiling. Already they are teaming up against her.

The sidewalk isn't wide enough for three. Kathryn keeps getting edged into the wet grass until she drops back behind the other two, and then can't follow what they are talking about. Something captivating. Kathryn scans for large objects she might duck behind and disappear while the other two walk on, oblivious.

After a block or so, Emily falls back to join Kathryn, then Chris does the same, and then the whole shuffle starts again.

On the bus, there aren't enough seats together and they are quickly separated—Kathryn and Chris herded to the back, Emily stranded up front. They're an hour ahead of schedule and it's rush hour, thanks to Emily.

Kathryn feels for Chris. She always hates to see one of his plans unravel. He puts so much into them and then can't let go. It's painful to watch, and Kathryn cannot at this moment bring herself to look at his tender face and what might be happening there.

Kathryn can see Emily at the front of the bus. She is talking with a chatty old walrus in a fishing hat. Emily lowers her ear to his mouth and listens for some time, then she says something directly into the old man's ear. A gummy smile spreads across his face. Kathryn watches them charm each other for twenty blocks. She can talk to people, this one. This is not someone with a list of conversation topics in her pocket.

Kathryn turns now to face Chris. His eyes are closed, his back very straight.

Sorry about your date, Kathryn says.

He smiles and opens his eyes, gives her a kiss on the cheek. It'll be fine, he says, his eyes closing again. He appears to be solving a puzzle in his head, like there are little sliding tiles behind his eyelids. He seems good, actually. Adaptable. But also, a little, like a Chris that Kathryn doesn't know.

At the restaurant, Chris and Emily confer over every item on the menu. Chris seems very invested in the options for someone who only ever orders the aloo gobi.

Kathryn watches Emily. How she gazes at Chris, full on. How she plops her menu down every time they land on a new appetizer or entrée, as if each dish were a Shakespearean tragedy they might discuss at some length. Emily's hair is going on greasy and exquisitely dishevelled. She talks out of one side of her mouth, which could be adorable or irritating.

Kathryn imagines that mouth pressed up against Chris's. At first that feels tolerable. It looks like a clean mouth. Kathryn pictures the mouths opening slightly, pulling at each other with little nibbles and tugs. Now a wave of nausea rolls in and Kathryn backs the mouths apart. She holds them there for a moment, separated, then eases them together again, trying to find the edge of nausea.

Emily is saying something to her.

Kathryn, you're a vegetarian, right?

I eat mostly vegetarian.

If I order veggies, do you want to share?

Sure, Kathryn says. She feels woozy. She has found the edge of nausea.

Emily decides on channa masala, which is in truth Kathryn's favourite, leaving Kathryn to order saag paneer. The words sound full of sorrow when she says them out loud to the waiter: saag paneer.

Chris is different with Emily, but how? That's what Kathryn is trying to figure out. With Emily, he orders the vindaloo. And he keeps touching his face. When he listens to Emily, he rests his fingertips on his mouth like he is trying to keep something in.

With Emily, he tells his same stories differently. The facts are unchanged, but they're given different weights. The tone shifts and wraps itself around Emily, more sensual, more mysterious, but without the familiar ache and ambivalence that had so spoken to Kathryn when she first heard these stories.

When he tells Emily about the whales and his family asleep in their tents, Kathryn can see the whales, really see them for the first time, the water rolling down their glistening skin. She can feel the little boy's heart filling with a sense of belonging. But she can't taste the sadness of the story. It isn't being told for her.

With Emily, there are openings in the stories like crevices in coral. Emily reaches into these openings, sometimes up to her shoulder, and pulls things out. Emily says things like, But why didn't you wake them?

I don't know, Chris says.

What would have happened? she asks.

Chris looks at Emily and blinks. Seven times he blinks.

It would have given my mom another reason to love my dad, he says. It had been their one and only camping trip as a family, his dad's idea, and it had been going badly. Chris didn't want his dad to get credit for the whales.

Chris and Emily study each other in the glow of this insight. Kathryn wonders if the food will ever arrive.

So Emily, what is it you do? Kathryn says, sounding, she realizes, like someone's uncool mom.

Oh god, says Emily and laughs, and it seems like she would like to leave it there.

But for some reason, Kathryn cannot leave it there.

Emily has jobs.

On weekdays, she walks a springer spaniel named Cornelius whose owners Emily has, to this day, never met. She inherited the job from a friend, she says, who had never met them either, but every afternoon there is a fresh twenty-dollar bill on the dining room table. On weeknights, she sometimes babysits a six-year-old boy whose parents are in a jazz trio called Tall Weather Theory. Chris nods, like he has heard of them. Maybe he has. He's always making Kathryn CDs full of undiscovered new bands and obscure old ones he knows she'll love. On Mondays, Emily cleans the house of a woman with three small children and a clinical depression. Emily found her depression workbook under the bed, incompletely filled in. The house is always frustratingly clean when Emily arrives and Emily suspects, she says solemnly, that her real job is being there to find the body, if it ever comes to that, before the children get home from school. There are other jobs, too, that Emily lists, but Kathryn can't hold on to them.

So are you an artist of some sort? Kathryn says.

An artist?

Or something. Are you juggling all these jobs so you can do something else?

No, that's what I do.

Oh. Cool, says Kathryn and feels awful. There is a terrible moment of no one saying anything.

I'd like to be a house cleaner, Chris says into the silence. He'd be good, too, Kathryn thinks. She abdicated most of the cleaning to him years ago.

I think I might use the washroom, Emily says.

Did that sound mean? Kathryn says.

I don't know, says Chris. Were you trying to be mean?

I was trying to get to know her. I was trying to show an interest in this person that you think is so amazing.

Two waiters appear with the entrées and spend some time arranging and rearranging them on the table. Kathryn waits. When the waiters retreat, she speaks.

You do know what I mean, though?

No, says Chris. I don't know.

Think about Tight Mike, Kathryn says.

Tight Mike had been a semi-acquaintance from their film society days who had spent three years on his kitchen floor making a stop-motion re-enactment of *The Shining* funded entirely by pharmaceutical trials and occasional night shifts at the rendering plant. When Chris and Kathryn eventually saw his strangely lyrical film, they wished they had invited him over for dinner as he got thinner and paler.

Or what about Rebecca, says Kathryn, or Hector before he started teaching. They had known a lot of people, years ago, who were doing one thing so they could pursue another thing.

I think she's just living her life, Chris says.

The waiters are back with rice and various chutneys. Again there is much maneuvering and shuffling of the little silver dishes. What does Chris mean, just living her life? Does he think Kathryn is not living her life? Is he thinking his own life might be more lived? And how did Kathryn end up in the wrong here? She gave him what he wanted. She put her feelings aside. And now she's the selfish one?

Are you angry? Kathryn says when the waiters finally leave. She isn't sure what angry looks like on Chris. Usually, whenever it looks like they might disagree about something, Chris takes her side.

I just don't know what we're doing, he says.

They wait for Emily, their arms at their sides, and watch the food steaming.

Emily returns buoyant and unruffled. Everyone tastes everything and says something.

So how did you two get together? Emily wants to know, once they are eating in earnest.

Chris tells a nice story about how they'd been friends for a long time first, how they met at the film society where he was the weekend projectionist, and where Kathryn came in most Saturdays to copy-edit the next month's program, and how sometimes when she was done for the night she'd come up to the projection booth and watch the last hour of the movie with him through the little square window, though mostly they had talked, and how they had to whisper in the booth, making everything they said to each other for the first year feel like a secret.

Emily is listening so hard she barely eats. She has many questions. Did you guys know right away? Why did Kathryn want to watch from the booth in the first place? What did you talk about up there?

I didn't know right away, says Chris. Did you?

Kathryn shakes her head no. She had thought Chris too good to be hers.

Chris tells Emily that the reason that they didn't know right away is that they were both in relationships, messy relationships with people who didn't like them for who they were, and that that's what they talked about in the booth. They would sit on the floor and listen to each other and say, You deserve better, until they gradually convinced each other that was true.

We rescued each other, Chris says.

That's what Chris always says: They rescued each other. The fact is, he rescued her. All she did for him was open an unlocked door.

It was Chris who sat on the floor of the booth and listened to her complain about Geoffrey. How Geoffrey withdrew his enthusiasm for something as soon as Kathryn began to enjoy it, how he used self-improvement as a weapon, how he drove away her friends with a quiet contempt, how he insisted on double-checking the deadbolt because one time she had forgotten to lock it, how he convinced her that it was dumb to like Sarah McLachlan, that it was immoral to take long showers, that it was pathetic to sleep so much, and that it was in every way wrong to be the way she was.

Chris had never whispered a hard word about Penny.

Chris just listened and said, That's not okay, and told Kathryn that she was amazing and deserved to be with someone amazing. It was Chris who said, once, That sounds like abuse.

But Kathryn said no. Because she didn't feel entitled to that word, though it was constantly there in her head.

Then, to her surprise, Chris said okay. He did not come at her with a dictionary. He did not drag her to a website that would prove he was right. He said okay, and he put his hand on the floor next to hers.

Two months later when Geoffrey called some woman on the TV a dumb twat, Kathryn got up and walked out of their apartment and walked downtown and walked into the projection booth and said, Can we go somewhere?

They got a hotel room, Chris and Kathryn, and spent the night on top of the covers. The next day, Chris went alone to Kathryn's apartment with a key and a list and got her clothes, her reference books, and her journals and brought them to the hotel.

That night, they played canasta like old ladies and a week later they moved into an apartment together—broke, friendless, and in love. They were driven out of the film society, where most of their former friends rallied around Penny. But there would be new friends, a new life. And whenever people would ask how they got together, Chris would say, as he is saying now, that they rescued each other, although what he really thinks,

Kathryn is not sure. They don't discuss it much. They each have their own ways of feeling bad about how it happened.

Well fuck those people, says Emily.

Kathryn laughs, a loud surprised honk.

No seriously, Emily says. Fuck them. She raises her water glass to toast. Chris hoists his, then Kathryn does, too.

To people who love you for who you are, Emily says. They clink glasses, the three of them.

Chris *has* loved Kathryn for who she is, for nine years now. He has joined her in her long showers. He has valued her penny-pinching. He has admired her ability to sleep in. He has loved her in a way that she didn't know was possible.

And now he needs this one thing that he doesn't even know he needs. Something to do with this girl with the clean-looking mouth and the astute questions. When was the last time Sharon asked questions like that? This girl who makes time speed up and slow down. The restaurant is emptying already. This girl who makes Chris come alive in ways Kathryn has never seen: Chris is proposing now that they go somewhere for coffee. He doesn't like coffee, she knows. He doesn't like being up this late. But he doesn't want this night to be over. He needs something. Is Kathryn going to be the person to stand in his way?

Chris is in the restroom, possibly going over his notes. Kathryn and Emily look at each other across the stained tablecloth. There is still time, Kathryn thinks, to say something. To be magnanimous. To get the upper hand.

Emily is lifting single fennel seeds from a tiny bowl and placing them in her mouth.

He really likes you, Kathryn says at last.

I really like him, Emily says.

Kathryn watches Emily's mouth move as she says this and imagines it, again, pressed up against Chris's, fresh with fennel.

What movie were you going to watch? Emily asks.

I hadn't actually picked one.

Ah, says Emily. Another seed disappears behind her smile.

You didn't know this was a date, did you? Kathryn says.

I knew it was a date, Emily says. I think it's going great, don't you?

OCTOBER

CHAPTER 5

Second Date

It's not a date.

Chris doesn't like to call it a date. It's a walk. They're going on a walk, he and Emily. And along the route are seven of Chris's favourite used bookstores. And in between the bookstores, seven specific restaurants, each with a particular item on a theme. He has it all planned. From the salad rolls at Mekong Palace to the cherry cream tarts at Leo's Floral & Sweets, it's a seven-course meal in finger foods.

That's a date, Kathryn says as he's putting on his shoes.

We're hanging out, says Chris.

Mm-hm.

We're getting to know each other.

Yeah. On a date.

She teases him like this, needles him almost, which is new. It unnerves him. Twice this week he has decided to call the thing off, whatever it is, this thing with Emily. Just go back to before, when he and Emily would bump into each other sometimes, coming out of a store or crossing the street, and then Chris would spend a week regaining his equilibrium. They could go back to that. He'd survive. Everyone would survive.

But then Kathryn sells it to him again. How she wants him to do this, at least once, without her in tow. How it feels important.

And the fact is they are kissing more these days, Chris and Kathryn, since their dinner with Emily. There has been more pawing and pouncing, more lather in the shower, more love attacks.

I'll be back by eleven, Chris says. It's almost two thirty now.

Kathryn grabs his nose and holds it.

Don't set a time, she says. Just come home.

Emily is already at the park when Chris crests the hill. He recognizes her from blocks away, before she is even recognizable, really. But there she is, an unmistakable dot amongst the smudges.

He angles across the park toward her. It is early October and children are playing in coats and boots.

Emily is sitting on a bench by the jungle gym. A wobbly child is carrying pebbles from the playground, one by one, and handing them to Emily. Why thank you, Emily says when the boy drops each small offering into her hand. The boy smiles and charges off to find another.

Chris sits down on the bench, off to one side, like a stranger. He doesn't say any of the things he'd been planning to say. They don't speak at all, in fact, but sit and watch the little boy select the perfect pebble and run back to hand it to Emily. People want to give her things, Chris thinks, and wishes now that he had brought some small something to put in her hand.

Why thank you, Emily says. Do you think my friend here could have one? she says, and gestures over to Chris. The boy looks at Chris and considers. He seems uncertain, but totters away and, at some length, selects a stone he considers fitting.

Why thank you, Chris says when the boy returns with the find. Chris makes a point of admiring the pebble, which is in fact quite beautiful, but the boy has already run off in search of more.

Should we go? Emily says. She hops to her feet and throws her arms around Chris. Hi, she says.

They head out of the park, heading west. He has a bottle of champagne in his backpack in case they make it to the ocean.

They talk without economy, nothing saved for later, nothing portioned out. Chris wishes he could write everything down, so that later he could go back over each moment and take it apart like a clock.

Emily talks about growing up in San Francisco and what brought her here. (A train, she says in the end.) Chris talks about growing up in a small town and the sister who never left. They talk about Emily's parents, who are still in love, and Chris's, who maybe never were.

They talk about Halloween—her love of it and his dread. It is only the first week of October, and already some of the houses have cobwebs and skeletons showing. Chris despises it, Halloween, and has since he was a kid—the gore and malevolence, the marauding teens, the bottle rockets. But even as Chris is listing his grievances, he finds himself warming to the holiday, because Emily said, simply, I like it.

They talk about ghosts and whether they believe. (They do.) They talk about music and promise each other mixes. They talk about the spinal problems of basset hounds and the nasal passages of pugs. And how did anyone figure out that rhubarb was edible? Did someone say, Well the leaves are deadly, now let's try eating the stalks?

Sometimes a single sentence will branch out in a dozen different directions, and yet Chris and Emily follow them all, looping around, dropping nothing. Chris feels breathless and switched on like a current.

All week, Chris has been telling himself that once he gets to know Emily, as she becomes more defined and specified and real, he will be able to think about her reasonably, without chest pain.

What if the opposite is happening?

In the first bookstore, Emily wanders away and Chris loves that. He is embarrassed for couples who proceed side by side through the shelves, reading the odd title out loud and making their little commentaries. The joy is to go your separate ways, to find your separate treasures, and then bring them to each other.

Today, Chris finds pearls in every section. Science. Religion. Biography. Everything looks good today. All subjects seem possible and necessary. He keeps culling the books he is carrying, keeping only the best, replacing the perfect book with an even more perfect book until the stack is a work of art.

When he finds Emily, she is sitting in a wicker chair with a cat on her lap. The animal is in some sort of rapture, purring like an outboard motor.

Did you find anything? Emily says.

Chris shows her the titles one by one. The cat turns its head as if to look, but does not open its eyes. Chris reads a line or two from each book, and he and Emily talk about why he picked it, what makes it special.

Then Chris puts the books back where he found them.

You aren't going to buy any? Emily says.

I don't think so, he says. He doesn't feel right buying books if Emily isn't getting any.

Outside it is starting to spit.

They eat with their hands, like gods. Tiny foods tucked into other foods, unknown pleasures pressed into pockets and fried. Morsels, Emily says. Whenever a plate is placed before them, she says: Mmmmmorsels. Chris thinks it is the best sequence of sounds he has ever heard in a single word.

In the next bookstore, Emily strikes up a conversation with the owner. Chris can hear them from the back of the shop where he is looking at dictionaries. For twenty minutes, Chris pretends to look at dictionaries, but in fact, stands listening to Emily and how she talks to people and the way she is in the world.

It isn't small talk. It's actual conversation, generous and curious and real. It fascinates Chris, it attracts him, but he does not move to join in. Rather he hides, lingers in the back of the shop longer than he wants to, waiting for the encounter to die down so he can emerge safely and not be introduced.

What Chris does not want Emily to know about him, not yet, is that he doesn't generally talk to people. He can talk to

Kathryn, of course. And Emily now. He could talk with them all day and night. But other people? Most people make Chris tired.

His sister says he's superior, that he thinks he's too good for people. But Chris likes people. He likes the owner of this store, whose name he knows is Carol. Carol hosts readings every couple of months—quiet, cozy affairs with folding chairs and tea—and Chris admires her knowledge of the authors' other books and her insightful introductions. Chris reads her blog. He listens in when she recommends books to other, chattier customers. But he's never spoken to Carol. What would he say?

He doesn't need to pal around with Carol the way some customers do. He wants to nod politely when he comes in, and again when he leaves, and otherwise just think well of each other.

But Chris wants, also, to be like Emily. Or at least to stand beside Emily and feel the gravitational force of her. So Chris does, at last, wrest himself from the dictionaries and walk out into the open. Emily introduces him immediately.

Carol, this is my good friend Chris.

Carol reaches out and shakes Chris's hand. I see you in here all the time, Carol says.

That's true, Chris says stupidly.

Your store is his favourite, Emily says. He's been taking me on the rounds.

Carol smiles fondly at Chris, as if they are childhood pen pals who've finally met in old age. She asks if he saw the Barthelmes over in New Arrivals. (He hadn't, what with hiding.) Chris asks how the Kevin Chong reading went last week, and Carol lights up with funny anecdotes. She says if there's ever anything Chris is after, he should tell her, and she'll put it aside for him. Chris can think of several things right off.

They go on like this for fifteen minutes and it's not unendurable. Now he'll have to think of something to say to Carol every time he comes into the store.

They eat a mouthful here, another mouthful a mile away. They chew slowly. They lick sauce from little saucers.

In ten years, Emily says, I will still remember every single bite.

They tip extremely well and leave hungry. It feels good to carry this hunger along, with just the tickle of satisfaction in their mouths.

In the back of another bookstore, Chris discovers a cloth-bound copy of Charlotte Brontë's *Villette*. It's $100. It has a green satin ribbon to hold your place and wide creamy margins. Emily finds Chris there just holding it.

It's Kathryn's favourite novel, Chris says. Have you read it?

Emily shakes her head.

It's good, Chris says. Supposed to be her best.

What's it about? Emily says.

Chris tries to remember. He has read it. Kathryn brought her copy to the projection booth, years ago, along with some curry noodles, and left it for him to read. Chris had loaned her *Reasons to Live* the week before. This was back at the very beginning of what they would later regard as their courtship, when they were urgently handing each other beloved novels and favourite albums.

It's about a woman, Chris says. He wants to say more about the woman—Lucy? Sylvie?—and about her particular situation, but he can't bring it into focus. He knows there was longing and suffering, but for Chris, when he read it, the book was about

Kathryn. It was about Kathryn being with a man who didn't like her and not knowing what to do.

Chris remembers Kathryn talking about the book, excitedly, both before he'd read it and after, and using the word *indefatigable*. And he remembers wondering what it would be like to kiss someone who used the word *indefatigable*.

Are you going to get it for her? Emily says.

Her copy is falling apart, he says. He can't put the book down.

You should get it.

Chris holds the book up to his nose. It smells like a book Kathryn should have.

At the Indonesian place, the staff seems tense around Emily. The venerable old woman who fills water glasses will not look at Emily and will not smile at Chris. The woman has always smiled at Chris, at first because he drank so much water, which pleased her and gave them a silent bond, and later because he began to surprise her with diligently-practised phrases in Indonesian. Thank you. You are very kind. I always feel thirst.

Chris and Kathryn have been coming here since Kathryn was still in grad school. They were here last week for Chris's birthday. Normally, the owner comes out to welcome them and talk for some minutes about her son who is in university now and might become a pediatrician. She'll say something like, Do you remember, we were so worried about him? Because when Chris and Kathryn first started coming here, the son was in high school and getting into trouble. Maybe drugs?

Tonight he and Emily are not welcomed by the owner, or by anyone.

Their one appetizer takes forty minutes to appear, though the restaurant is empty. Chris imagines the people in the kitchen talking about him and Emily, using words he will never find in his Indonesian dictionary.

When the owner does come out, it is with the bill.

And how is your other friend? she says, as Chris signs the receipt. She is at home?

Outside the restaurant, three men start hugging Emily, and she, them. They all seem overjoyed to have found each other. Chris steps back, out of the way. They are huddled under the awning. It is really raining now.

Emily introduces the men to Chris.

This is Chris, she says. She pulls him into the circle. Chris works in a film archive, she says.

The men are impressed by this. They nod approvingly. Chris has already forgotten their names.

Hey, what are you up to right now? the one man asks Emily.

We're just hanging out, Emily says.

Chris wishes now that they were not just hanging out, that there was another word for what they are doing, a stronger word they could use with these men so they would understand.

You guys should come to the Make Room, the man is saying. He says a friend of theirs—of Emily and these men—is doing something at an open mic.

This friend of theirs is a genius, Emily tells Chris, and could probably be a star, but he won't do the same piece twice. You have to see it the one time, or you never see it.

What kind of stuff does he do? Chris asks.

The friends debate this for some time, inconclusively.

You should come, the man says. You should both come.

I don't think so, guys. Chris made this whole plan for us.

Now Chris is ashamed of his plan. His plan is all wrong. It should be more spontaneous. It should be a non-plan.

The man is working on Emily.

I don't know, she says. Then turning to Chris: What do you think?

Sure, Chris says, all spontaneous.

Emily is silent for a moment. Everyone watches her think.

No, she says, I think we're going to do our thing.

The men look disappointed. Then more hugging.

Hey, any word from Chris? says the one man.

Emily shrugs. He calls, she says.

The man nods. Well, say hi.

The men head off in one direction, regrettably the same direction that Chris and Emily must go. They trail behind the men for several awkward blocks. Chris considers changing course, abandoning the remaining bookstores. Everything is all wrong. He shouldn't be here. He should be home with Kathryn. If Chris was home right now, he and Kathryn would be brushing their teeth, taking forever as usual, because they can't stop telling each other all the little things that happened to them today. He would rub Kathryn's feet until she fell asleep, and then lie beside her and read his book, or maybe start *Villette* again. Chris knows how to be with Kathryn. He knows how to be what Kathryn needs.

And let's be honest: He doesn't have the capacity to be with Emily. He could never make her happy. He is sure the Other Chris would've said yes to unexpected performance art. The Other Chris would have grasped the hands of those men and cared to learn their names. And Emily should have that. Emily should have someone who is vital and outgoing and full of life, not stunted and broken.

How you doing? Emily says.

Good, Chris says. Great.

Yeah? She slows them to a stop with a hand on his arm.

I feel a little off, he says.

Here, she says, and pulls him into the doorway of a darkened dry cleaners. She sits him on the step and stands in front of him, then digs her thumbs hard into his face. It's a welcome pain. Her hands are small and powerful. She works slowly on the ridge of his eye sockets, his cheekbones, his eyebrows. He can feel things shifting around inside.

The people in that restaurant think I'm cheating on Kathryn, he says finally.

Emily sits down beside him. She is looking at him, Chris can tell, but he cannot look back. She takes his hand and laces her fingers into his.

Do you think you're cheating? she says.

He sits with the question while it accumulates around him. The voices of the men are distant now, almost gone.

Okay, Emily says, who are the people affected by this?

By what?

By you and me. This. Emily waves her hand to take in the little stoop and awning and them sitting there. Who does this affect?

Kathryn, he says. It is Kathryn he is thinking about, above all. And you, he adds. And me.

Anyone else?

Chris thinks. It seems like he's forgetting someone.

How about those people in the restaurant? Emily says.

Chris laughs, once, through the nose. It feels good to listen to her.

So, she says, there are three people who get a say in this.

Chris nods.

Let's go in order, she says. What does Kathryn want?

I don't know.

What does she say?

She said it's a date.

Okay.

Chris looks up now to catch Emily's expression. He notices she does not deny it is a date.

What else? Emily says.

She said go. Have fun.

Alright, next up, Emily says, what do *you* want?

I want to not be an asshole.

Oh my friend, she says, and she puts her head on his shoulder. Her weight feels good on his bones.

Do you want to head home? she says.

Maybe.

They sit on the steps and watch cars driving too fast in the rain and people walking by in twos and threes. Chris keeps hoping for one of these people to turn and notice them sitting here like this, holding hands, on a date, but nobody does.

Come on, Emily says, pulling him to his feet. Walk me home.

They talk on the way home about being an asshole, about people they have wronged, about the objects they swallowed as children. They talk about Emily's brother who sometimes doesn't want to live.

They take turns asking each other questions. Chris asks, What do people misunderstand about you? Emily asks, What do you think you'll be like when you're really old? Chris asks, Do you know another Chris?

The Other Chris is a guy she knew—knows—a good guy, a musician, who decided it made more sense to just stay on tour.

He was your boyfriend? Chris says.

Not entirely.

But sort of?

We were seeing each other, Emily says. We dated.

They talk about who they have dated, about who made them the people they are, about who broke up with whom and why. It is cold and raining, but they are not miserable.

They stand in front of Emily's house for several minutes. The conversation subsides in waves like a tide rolling out. Then they're not talking anymore and there is an interval where it feels like something should happen. Chris wonders if they are going to kiss. Is that what he wants? He isn't sure that it is. Unless it's what Emily wants, and then he wants it more than anything.

Can we do this again? Emily says.

Yes, he says. After today, his calendar is blank.

She puts her arms around him and holds him.

I always call you, he says. Is that weird?

Should I call you?

You certainly could.

Then I will, she says.

Chris bounds the sixteen blocks home. He imagines himself living in a world where the phone rings and it's Emily.

CHAPTER 6

The Right Thing to Feel

I'll be back by eleven, Chris says.

I should hope so, Kathryn thinks. It's not even two thirty in the afternoon. What could they possibly do for almost nine hours on this non-date? Does Chris have nine hours of conversation mapped out in his little book? Can he even stay awake past ten anymore? It all seems unlikely, this eleven o'clock.

Still, Kathryn doesn't like the possibility that Chris might say eleven and then—through no fault of his own—come in at 11:05. He might be legitimately delayed. Someone could have a seizure on the sidewalk and Chris would stop to help. But then there would be these five minutes that would have to be dealt with, would have to be absorbed somehow, a concrete betrayal that can be measured in international units.

Or worse, that he's right on time, but he's right on time because he said to Emily: I wish I didn't have to leave. I'd rather stay here with you, but I promised Kathryn.

Better to be late than to come when you don't want to come. Better to not set a time at all.

Besides, he has already said eleven. Once Chris says he'll do something, he does it. Even when you pretend it's not important. Even when you sincerely release him from obligation, he is unswerving.

So it's easy to say, Don't set a time. It's easy to be generous and unconcerned. Because you know he'll be home by eleven.

By seven o'clock, Kathryn has watched a toxic amount of sitcoms. She can feel deposits forming in her fatty tissue—the smirking gags, the cheap innuendo—settling in and becoming part of her like mercury in a slow-moving tuna.

She had planned to work all afternoon, ideally all evening. She needed the time. She has had this manuscript on her desk for a month already, and not one word of the index is done. The thing goes to the printer in less than a week. Impossible. Still, a lot could be achieved in nine hours.

Instead, she had watched Chris disappear through the peephole and then sat down in front of the TV and turned on the worst show she could find.

Sitcoms, it turns out, have a lot of people going on first dates. These dates are usually disastrous, ha-ha. Kathryn let these episodes slosh around her and tried not to imagine things. Occasionally, though, a sitcom-date goes well, spectacularly well, and you know that this new character is going to be around for a while. Maybe a few episodes, maybe whole seasons. These good dates, Kathryn watched more closely. Were they genuinely good? Were the characters being true to themselves? Were they following the rules? If Chris and Emily were on that same date right now, would that be okay? Would Kathryn be okay?

She turns the TV off. The mockery and canned laughter hang in the room. She puts some pasta on to boil. She paces around the apartment. It feels small. She wants to move. She wants to sprint across the alley and have her friend still live there and still be that friend.

She calls Sharon on the phone.

Chris is on a date, Kathryn says.

A what?

With Emily.

There is a deadness on the line.

That fucking asshole, Sharon says.

No, I told him to.

Right, says Sharon. Told him how?

I told him to ask her out.

Jesus, Kathryn. Why the hell?

Kathryn doesn't answer. She is wondering if she might vomit. The smell of the pasta is filling the kitchen. She listens to the open line.

Do you want me to come over? Sharon says at last.

I'm fine, Kathryn says.

I'm coming over.

Don't.

Twenty minutes.

Bring wine, Kathryn says.

———

When she hangs up, Kathryn feels a slap of clarity. Why shouldn't she let Chris go on a date? They're adults. And it's *their* fucking relationship, not Sharon's. There are lots of ways to be in a relationship, Sharon, ways they don't put on TV. People are capable of amazing things. Kathryn could be capable of amazing things. She and Chris are smart, caring people who love each other. They can try things out, and if those things don't work, they can try something else, or go back to how they were before. Kathryn could call Chris right now and tell him to come home, and he would, if he had a cell phone. Kathryn could say, I need you to not see Emily ever again, and Chris would do it. He would erase Emily from his very thoughts. But Kathryn's not going to ask that, because that's not what love is, Sharon. Love isn't I love you so much that I need to possess you and control you and be the source of all your happiness. Love is I love you so much that I want you to have everything you need, even when it's hard for me. And besides, what would Kathryn and Chris be doing if he wasn't on a date right now? It's eight o'clock at night. They'd be in bed, reading. Kathryn doesn't even like the book she's in the middle of. And most of all, it's *her* goddamned relationship. So what gives Sharon—with her new bed and oatmeal sex—the right to tell Chris and Kathryn what they should or should not be doing on a Friday night?

Kathryn would like to yell at Sharon. Kathryn has never yelled at Sharon, not yet. But Kathryn also likes the idea of Sharon being here when Chris gets home, sitting with her at the kitchen table, relaxed and drinking and laughing and saying to Chris, How was your date? Was it disastrous-ha-ha? Was it cliff-hanger good? Kathryn likes the idea of hearing the succinct version that Chris would tell with Sharon in the room, hearing that version first, before he tells Kathryn every little thing.

At 8:37, Sharon texts:

> Stuck here.
> Can't come.
> Tomorrow?

You know what? No. Not tomorrow. She's not waiting around anymore. Kathryn is not going to sit here for two hours eating buttered pasta and waiting for her boyfriend to come home and tell her he still loves her. She is going to do something.

She is going to put on her jacket—the old one that Geoffrey said made her look like a man. She is going to open her front door and charge toward something.

This is good, Kathryn thinks. She is walking hard down Broadway. It's barely nine, but it feels like the middle of the night. The sun has been down for hours.

She used to stomp around this city all night. Before Chris, before Geoffrey. She was seventeen and emancipated. During the day, she plowed through correspondence courses from her old school district back home and at night she put on her thrift-store boots and this thick black jacket and would go out and watch people make choices, to see how people lived when they weren't afraid of God. Kathryn would take up a whole booth at late-night diners and eat plates of hash browns. She would let drunk men give her advice. She would wander down by the Cut where the graffiti artists would nod to her gravely and go about their work. She would put herself in the middle of things and see what would happen. Mostly nothing happened. Mostly people left her alone. By the time she started university, she'd been in the city for ten months and knew no one. She felt impervious.

This jacket, though, was never great in the rain. It's soaking through now.

There's an all-night place in the bus station where the old Kathryn used to go to drink cup after cup and let her clothes dry out. That's where the sidewalk is taking her now.

Kathryn takes a booth no one wants, back by the bathroom. She orders pie. There is an almost whole cherry pie under a plastic dome on the counter. It is exactly what the ritual requires. She holds each bite in her mouth, letting the filling run and pool under her tongue, and she thinks about food shortages. She thinks about people driven from their land by famine. She thinks about wheat left to rot in warehouses while people starve. She thinks about the man outside the bus station picking through garbage cans. So who is Kathryn to be unhappy? Who is she to sit here with pie in her mouth and say life is miserable? She has everything. She has more than anyone needs. And yet she is jealous? Greedy and grudging and unwilling to share? No, that must stop.

Kathryn is mapping that part of herself—honing in on that grasping, malignant part. She will find exactly where it is. Then she will cut it out by the roots. She knows how.

———

When Kathryn was little, she had wanted a kitten. There was a poster of a kitten at her dentist's. It said, Wake me when it's Friday. Kathryn didn't care about Fridays, but she loved the kitten, and thought about it all year, between checkups. She asked her mother if they could get a kitten. Kathryn's mother said kittens kill cats—Kathryn's mother had ideas about things—but that maybe, if Kathryn was good, they might get an old cat that no one else wanted. Kathryn had argued and pleaded because she wanted a kitten that would fit in a teacup like the one on the poster, until her mom said, That's it, and put her in the pastor's car and drove her to the town humane society and showed her all the animals in cages. Most of these cats, her mother said, will never have a home because nobody wants a grown cat, everybody wants a cute little kitten like you do. Her mother told her that if nobody adopted these cats this week, they'd be taken into a small metal room and killed. Her mother pointed to a windowless door that led somewhere. Kathryn had cried—broken down there, right on the linoleum—and her mother took her home and gave her vegetable broth and told her that crying didn't fix anything. Kathryn was seven.

The next day, Kathryn's mother was waiting for her after school and took her back to the humane society to show her the poor cats again and point out the ones that were missing. Kathryn begged to take home one of these poor cats—an old calico with a dent in his face—but her mother said no. I believe in your heart you still want a kitten, she said and dragged Kathryn home. For a week or more, they went back every day and came home empty-handed until one day there was a litter of kittens at the shelter and Kathryn couldn't stand to look at them. She was repelled by their cuteness.

That's how you cut something out by the roots. You figure out the right thing to feel, and you make yourself feel it.

Kathryn orders another piece of pie, coconut cream, just to enjoy this time. It's even better than the cherry. She didn't eat dinner. She feels a calm coming on. The world comes into focus around her. She admires the people in the diner with their own worries and joys. She peers right into their faces. Some look back, confused. She smiles.

Somewhere Chris and Emily are enjoying their time together. Kathryn can afford to be happy for them. That feeling exists inside her, like a seedling poking through the dirt. Kathryn can sit in this bus terminal all night and eat pie with these people and be happy because the person she loves is happy.

Condensation creeps up the windows.

Her placemat is a map from the bus company. A continent of lines and dots.

Anywhere in the country for $89, it says.

That can't be right. Kathryn looks for the fine print. $89 is nothing—an afternoon's work to go thousands of miles. She could get on the next bus—the 11:50—and wake up in one of those unlabelled dots between the other dots. Buy a toothbrush from a vending machine. Watch the towns go by until one feels right. Some town with two supermarkets and one high school where you can rent an apartment for $200. What's the smallest apartment there is? Is there something smaller than a bachelor? Kathryn would be willing to pay more for smaller. She'll get a job doing something in an office. Maybe the high school. And her co-workers will be people who grew up in the town, who've known each other since kindergarten, who rib each other and gossip, and Kathryn will listen and smile and let it nourish her, and on Fridays they will ask does she want to come out with them after work and she'll say, No, no, go without me, until someday they don't ask anymore, but she could still come if she wanted. How long would it take to run out the rest of her life? Thirty years? Surely no more than fifty. She'll shop at Safeway like everyone else and that'll be fine.

$89 is the advance purchase price, says Daniel at the ticket counter. Two weeks for those. To get on a bus tonight would be $389. Kathryn could do that. She has almost $1800 in her bank account. But $89 felt better.

Let me think about it, she says.

The 11:50 leaves in twenty minutes. Chris would be home by now. Kathryn can see him coming in, full of things to tell her, and finding the apartment empty.

She knows he would never recover. If the last thing known of Kathryn Louise Matzen was a bowl of uneaten noodles on the kitchen table, Chris would never let himself be happy again. He would be destroyed. And he truly is the best person she has ever known. Kathryn would have to get word to him somehow. And then she wouldn't really be disappearing at all.

Kathryn sits on a metal bench by Bay 8. It's too cold to rain now. She can see her breath. She enjoys feeling like one of the smokers, topping up before the trip, waiting until the last moment to climb those three steep steps.

Some of the young women look like they are wearing pyjamas. They carry large bed pillows and seem strangely proud.

Kathryn admires the empty-handed most of all. No luggage for them, no paperbacks. Just a ticket pointing some direction.

The 11:50 is half full. Kathryn has already picked out her seat, judging through the windows which ones are least desirable. Middle left, right over the wheel, directly under the ceiling-mounted TV.

The 11:50 leaves. The 12:20 arrives and departs. Buses come and go in flurries, followed by quiet intervals when the loading area is empty.

Kathryn doesn't want to go home. She is on the other side of tired now, which she hasn't felt since undergrad, keyed up and sharpened. She wants to stalk the city and watch people take chances, win or lose. She wants consequences.

But the old fearlessness she used to feel has leached out of her bones. How did she ever do it? How did she bomb around these streets and alleys and not sense the danger? Even the thought of walking home feels perilous tonight. So Kathryn stays put on the empty platform. She wonders if someone in a reflective vest will come out of the terminal and tell her to go home. Otherwise, she might sit here all night becoming her new self.

There is a scurrying movement, fast and close to the ground. Kathryn starts despite herself. How pathetic she is. Why be scared of a rat? She isn't scared of squirrels. And it's way over there, not close, not interested in her. Just a rat doing its thing. Kathryn forces herself to look right at the animal, to breathe calmly, to be with it, here in this big open space. It is shadow-coloured and drags its tail.

Then she sees the one near the garbage, the one by the drain, the one under the vending machine, the one on the ledge, the one by the puddle.

CHAPTER 7

Consequences

Chris has told Kathryn about everything. About holding hands on West Fourth; about the funny jokes they made; about maybe, possibly celebrating Halloween this year; about the moment they didn't kiss; about how Emily wants to do it again.

Kathryn is in the bathtub, submerged to her ears. She'd come home shivering, unable to get warm, and Chris, who'd had hours to imagine the worst, put her in a hot bath and sat on the bathmat offering to bring her tea or soup or anything. She'd laughed off his concern. She'd gone for a walk, she said. Tell me about your date, she said. And so he has told her everything.

Well, that sounds pretty wonderful, Kathryn says now. I'm happy for you. And she turns and gazes into his face and smiles serenely. Then she looks back at the tile. She twists the hot water faucet with her toes and lets the water run for a while. It is three in the morning. She seems unusually contented.

She is paving over her feelings, Chris can tell. He has seen her do it before, like with Geoffrey in the end. She never talked about Geoffrey those days at the hotel. She didn't cry or rage. She played cards and stared at the TV and made passable conversation, and then it was like Geoffrey had never happened.

Are you upset with me? Chris says.

Of course not, she says. Again that smile.

Is there anything I can do?

I need sleep, she says.

She pulls the plug with her foot and the water starts to groan out.

They lie beside each other in postures of sleep.

Kathryn will never ask it, but Chris is forbidding himself to ever see Emily again. It is unforgivable to make Kathryn suffer like this. He can feel it coming off her like heat radiating from an infection. Chris will phone Emily in the morning and tell her that it's impossible. He will say that he is sorry, that it is all his fault, that if it was only his own happiness at stake, he could be brave and daring and unshrinking, but that he can't live with hurting the people he loves, he can't. And Emily will listen open-heartedly and will accept it with a compassion and kindness that will make Chris love her still more. Oh crap, he loves her.

Chris can already feel his connection with Emily starting to evaporate. He'll have nothing to prove that this thing between them was ever there. No photo-booth strip of them in the clothes they wore. No carnival coin with their names stamped into the soft metal. He should have kissed her when he had the chance. He'd had permission.

———

In the stillness, Chris can hear each second scraping by. He wonders how long it will feel like this, in human years.

Day to day, not seeing Emily won't be that hard to accomplish. Chris can avoid the places Emily goes in the world, find another laundromat. He can stop his fingers from dialing her number. It's easy to control his hands and feet. But what does he do with the feelings? Pave over them, like Kathryn does? Or just pretend, as they are pretending now to be asleep? You can't live like that, Chris thinks. It's inhuman.

He is up and out of bed. There is no sleep in this room.

Do you want breakfast? he says.

Yes, says Kathryn. She kicks off the covers.

Chris scrambles the last of the eggs and gives most of them to Kathryn. He settles in with toast.

We need groceries today, Kathryn says.

They're out of everything. They usually go grocery shopping on Friday nights, when everyone else is at the discotheque. That's what Kathryn likes to say: when everyone else is at the discotheque.

They talk about the things they need—lemons, greens, dish soap—the things they always need.

I'd like to hang out with Emily again, Chris says.

You already said you would.

I mean, I'd like to keep hanging out with her.

Well, do.

Kathryn carries her plate to the sink and starts scrubbing it. Chris follows her.

You're saying it doesn't bother you?

I'm the one who told you to do it.

But does it bother you?

Kathryn sighs. I'm fine, she says, though Chris can see she is not. She's hardening where she stands. He wants to enfold her. He wants to comfort her and carry her to safety. But he also wants to get at something, now, before the concrete sets.

And what if I want more? Chris says.

More how?

What if I want to see her twice a week? Three times a week?

Then that's what we'll do.

How about every day? Is there anything that would upset you?

Chris, you should do whatever you have to do.

Great, he says.

There is a heaviness in the room. The refrigerator is making its sound.

So what do we do now? Chris says.

We get groceries.

It's five in the morning, K.

We'll go to Safeway.

Safeway, it turns out, doesn't open until seven on Saturdays. They sit on a dry patch of pavement by the entrance and lean against the wall, delirious with exhaustion.

They talk about the holidays looming up. Chris's mother has been threatening to come spend Christmas with them for a change, which has everyone nervous. Mom doesn't travel. And besides, she has the Christmas stuff; Chris and Kathryn have nothing. Not an ornament, not a cookie cutter.

I guess we'll get some, Kathryn says. Kathryn likes Christmas.

Oh wait, says Chris. He has just remembered *Villette*, stowed away in his backpack. He hands it to Kathryn, wrapped as it is in a paper bag.

Kathryn pulls the book from the sack and holds it in both hands, not opening it. She doesn't say anything, just stares at it. Then she lifts the book to her nose and breathes deeply. God, he loves her.

She leans into him. The press of her is reassuring.

Where did you find this? she says.

Last night. At Fuller's.

Kathryn nods.

They sit like this, half awake, while the parking lot fills with the smell of baking bread. People start to pull into parking spaces here and there and sit in their cars. Chris can hear the patter of news radio coming from a station wagon.

Is that what you really want? Kathryn says. To see her every day?

Chris considers this possibility, for the first time really. He does want Emily in his life like that, in that every day kind of way.

Kathryn exhales.

I'm not talking about sex, Chris says. Just that closeness.

And you don't see how that's a problem?

He doesn't see. He doesn't see how it's any different than having a best friend, like Kathryn has in Sharon.

It's not like that at all, Kathryn says.

It is. You talk to Sharon every day.

I don't.

I see you, Kathryn. I'm there right next to you when you do it.

Chris feels demented, hissing at each other, sleep starved in the halogen spill of a Safeway parking lot. The driver of the station wagon is eyeing them.

Look, Chris says, I don't need to date her. I don't need to kiss her, I don't need to hold hands, which by the way, you and Sharon do all the time—

Do you want to guess how many times I've talked to Sharon this week?

Well you used to, he says. You used to see her every single day.

Yes, but I'm not in love with Sharon.

They're almost yelling now. People are getting out of their cars. The automatic doors slide open and shut.

Inside, the size of the store disorients them. They keep having to trek from one end to the other, hunting for each item. None of the food looks like food.

Why did you tell me to ask her out? Chris wants to know.

Kathryn is contemplating frozen peas.

Why do it in the first place? he says.

Do we have to figure this out right now?

For months, you're all, Call her up, ask her out, get to know her. And then when I do you say, No, cancel that, stop everything.

I didn't say cancel anything.

It's not fair to me and it's not fair to Emily.

Oh, says Kathryn, her eyes flaring hot. Now we have to be fair to Emily?

She's part of this, too. What we do affects her.

No, Kathryn says. We're not having our first fight in nine years in a fucking Safeway. She puts the basket on the floor and strides down the frozen aisle to the exit.

They walk home in silence. It does them good.

———

They don't really know how to fight. They both keep inviting each other to go ahead and start. Mostly, they just sit there at the kitchen table waiting for it to happen.

Around mid-morning, Kathryn's cell starts ringing.

Is that Sharon? Chris asks.

Kathryn nods and sets the phone back down on the table. They listen to it ring until it stops.

Why are we doing this? Chris says.

Kathryn shrugs.

I'm sure you had a reason.

People get crushes, Kathryn says. I get them all the time.

You don't date them.

Chris, you couldn't stop talking about her.

Kathryn's phone starts again.

Go ahead if you want, Chris says.

Kathryn nods, as if she might, but she doesn't move to answer. They watch the phone light up and go dark.

I wanted you to be happy, Kathryn says.

I *was* happy. Chris is exasperated. Who's happier than us? he says. Seriously, who do we know who's half as in love as us?

I know, Kathryn says. And it's true. Most of the people they know envy their relationship. You two are so good together, people say. You guys are the perfect couple.

So how would you feel if we decided to call it off? Kathryn says. The Emily thing.

Off-off?

Kathryn nods.

I'd be sad, but—

See, that's exactly what I don't want.

Kathryn's phone is ringing again.

Wow, Chris says, Sharon really wants to talk to you today. He isn't trying to score a point, but it does seem like Kathryn gets to talk to her best friend every day.

They try to conjure lunch from what they have in the house—ketchup, hazelnuts, cornmeal. They pull Kathryn's emergency can of tuna down from the top shelf and sit around it with two forks.

Tell me what you like about her, Kathryn says.

Chris doesn't know what it is exactly. It's like an instinct, some secret scent that says: Leave the ocean, brave salmon, and swim up this particular stream without knowing why. Or like those kids who start eating chalk or dirt or whatever, and people figure they're crazy, these kids, because why would anyone eat chalk, and then it turns out they have some mineral deficiency.

What's your particular deficiency? Kathryn says.

But it's not that. It's more like this new part of himself. Like if you'd lived in the same house all your life and then someone comes over to visit and they say, Where does this door go?, this door you'd never noticed, and when you open it, you find this whole floor you didn't know was there, all these rooms.

She makes you feel like a better person, Kathryn says.

A bigger person. More capacity.

Chris feels at this moment that he could do anything, and that Kathryn is there with him, excited for him. Then she is paving over again.

———

The phone rings, the landline now.

Probably Sharon, Chris says between rings. But it's Emily. Chris and Kathryn take turns listening to the message:

EMILY: Hi Chris. Hi Kathryn. It's Emily calling. And Chris, I'm not just calling because you said I never call you. It's totally coincidental—I just keep thinking of things I want to tell you. There's so many, I'm actually writing them down, but I don't have a fancy little book like yours, so I'm writing them on my hand and it's getting a little messy, so call me soon, okay? Hey, how did Kathryn like the book? Kathryn, how did you like the book? Chris was so excited about it. Okay, well. Call me when you can and maybe we can pick a day to do something. I have some ideas. Next time, I think I'm in charge. Okay. Can't wait to see you.

Kathryn says, And can you honestly tell me that it's not about sex? What if Emily wants to go snorkeling?

Years ago, Chris had compared having sex—wanting sex—to snorkeling. Chris has been snorkeling, he explained, and it was great. But it has never occurred to him to go again. Snorkeling just doesn't call to him the way other things do. But here's the thing: If someone Chris loved got a sudden yen to go snorkeling, if Kathryn, for instance, said, Hey Chris, I'd really love to go snorkeling with you this weekend, he'd be more than happy to go. Because he loves that person and he loves doing things with them. And once he got there, it would probably be fantastic, minnowing through the water and exploring the hidden world. Of course he would go snorkeling! But then he might not think about it for weeks or months until the flippers and mask were brought out again.

I don't even know if Emily wants that, he says.

But she might, Kathryn says. And then you might.

Chris can't say he won't.

The sun falls down. They order pizza and wait forever. Sharon phones eleven more times. Chris and Kathryn sit on the kitchen floor and start sentences. They look up sleep delirium on the computer. The food arrives at last and sits on the counter uneaten because now they are crying, and by the time Kathryn falls asleep, they are all but broken up.

It had never occurred to Chris that they might break up. He had never imagined that one day they'd be talking in the kitchen and the ground would open up between them and Kathryn would say, My life is on this side and what you need is on that side, and that he would stand there on his side and nod.

Chris is curled up beside her on the floor, close, but not touching. Not her hip resting against his, or the tips of his fingers tucked under the waistband of her underwear. After nine years of touching, it feels impossible that they could ever sleep so separate. He studies her slack face and tries to imagine them being strangers. Or worse, acquaintances, who have to recognize each other and then stand there trying to sort out how long it's been so they know where to start the summary: Living in Toronto now. Yes, two kids.

It's shameful. It's shameful for two people to love each other for so long and then decide to stop. The shame of it rears up and pulls him under.

———

They sleep past noon and wake up tender and aching. The floor has betrayed them.

They're in the shower when Chris wonders if they should still shower together.

I don't ever want to not be able to shower with you, Kathryn says, and they hold each other until the hot water runs out. They eat the sweating pizza and go back to bed, and when they wake up on Monday, they are more or less together.

NOVEMBER

CHAPTER 8

Aboutness

Kathryn is drawing pineapples on the pages of the fucking manuscript. Pineapples are the only thing she knows how to draw from memory, and she draws them well. She likes the spiky, repeating pattern.

Kathryn has told the publisher she is having a family emergency, which bought her another week with the fucking manuscript. She did not tell the publisher that the family emergency entailed sitting up all night discussing ways that she and her boyfriend might sleep with other people. She let the publisher think someone was dying.

Kathryn tries not to hate anyone. Where she grew up, even the word wasn't allowed in the house. But she hates Jeremiah Raelson, the idiot polymath who wrote this book. Kathryn has Googled him a couple times, looking for some personal insight that might help her get a handle on the manuscript, but it only made her hate him more. He has broken her brain with his terrible book.

So she's sitting there drawing pineapples in his margins when Emily rings the doorbell.

Kathryn can see through the curtain that it's Emily. Kathryn considers not being home. It's a Thursday afternoon. Who's to say Kathryn's not out meeting a client?

Kathryn opens the door. There is a dog with Emily, the one she walks, presumably. He's sitting on his bottom like a good dog, looking up at Kathryn expectantly.

Chris is at work, Kathryn says, which Emily surely knows. Chris works nine to five; it's not a hard schedule to remember.

We came to see you, Emily says.

The dog's tail is starting to scoot his rump back and forth on the porch.

I wanted to see if you'd take a walk with us, Emily says.

Listen, Kathryn says, I'm talked out.

We don't have to talk about any of that stuff.

God, what else is there? Kathryn says, and Emily laughs like this is a wise joke. But seriously, that stuff is all Kathryn talks about anymore. She spends her days locked in dread silence with this fucking manuscript and her nights talking interminably with Chris, vivisecting their relationship.

I have this deadline, Kathryn says, and she waves her hand toward the manuscript on the other side of the room.

Emily nods like she understands. The dog is adorable, though. On principle, Kathryn's heart is closed to purebreds, but this is an old dog. Kathryn can see the beginnings of cataracts in his cloudy brown eyes. She squats down to say hello, to touch the soft fur behind his ears, the curls on his chest. He is genuinely happy to see her. Kathryn can feel his breath on her face. She likes the smell.

You might work better after a walk, Emily says.

Cornelius walks between them all the way to the dog park, his tail smacking their thighs. He looks up at them every couple of blocks, first at Emily, then at Kathryn, always in that order.

So what's it about, Emily says. The book.

But that's the problem—as far as Kathryn can see, the book isn't about anything. An index is a prediction, she hears herself telling Emily, a prediction of everything a reader might someday want to know. But Kathryn can't find anything in this book that a reasonable person would ever want to know.

This is terrible conversation, Kathryn knows. She's holding forth. Venting, really. But Emily seems interested—she keeps asking questions—and it makes Kathryn feel better to talk about something she really knows.

But isn't the worst book in the world still about something? Emily asks.

So Kathryn tries to describe the book to Emily, tries to address this lay-question of aboutness, and as she does, she finds herself having to make the book more elusive and confounding than it actually is, because as Kathryn is describing it, the book is opening up before her like a puzzle box. She sees how to index it. She could sit down and do it right now. She can see, too, that she was wrong about the book. This book is no shittier than any of the other shitty books she has worked on—just one more piece of civilization for the landfill. She doesn't hate Jeremiah Raelson. She hates her job.

———

At the park, Emily produces a tennis ball from her coat pocket and they take turns throwing it for Cornelius. Kathryn throws farther than Emily and this pleases Kathryn. She throws as hard as she can every time. Cornelius hurtles after the ball and returns it to their feet with real urgency. It's fun, actually, for all three of them.

The park is mostly empty, save for some soccer players, way at the other end. They're running drills, cheering each other on.

Impressive clouds are sliding across the sky, making the park bright one moment, almost warm, then dark and cold, now divided down the center, a hard, sharp shadow moving across the grass. Cornelius bounds into the shadow after the ball and emerges squinting into the light.

But how can you predict? Emily says, still on the index. How can you know in advance what any one person might want to know?

It's easy, Kathryn says. What's a book you've read recently?

Emily shrugs, like this might be a rhetorical question.

Any book, Kathryn says. Non-fiction.

Emily bends down to get the ball. I'm not a strong reader, she says, and she stands up and takes several steps forward to hurl the ball deep into the heart of the park.

Kathryn recognizes this language. It's something you might write in a student's file: Not a strong reader. But you don't say it to the child.

Cornelius is wearing himself out, but he won't quit. He still barrels after the ball at top speed, but then he plops himself down at the far end of the throw and pants heavily, and blinks long blinks—the ball held down with one paw—before trotting back. He'll go forever like this.

Kathryn and Emily sit down on a bench. Over at the far end of the park a woman is pacing back and forth and calling out some name—Aisha, maybe—over and over. Kathryn has a sick feeling about this. Aisha is not a dog's name.

The woman is getting louder now, more frantic. The soccer players have stopped their drills and are looking around. That's what everyone is doing now—looking left and right and back and front, but there are no children in this place. Kathryn can see the whole park from where she is and there's nowhere to hide, even if you were terribly small.

The woman is shrieking now, and the soccer players are rushing over to her, but she bats them away, veers off in a new direction, and then stalks out of the park crying out the name.

That's so awful, Emily says. The park is filling again with the ambient roar of the city and they sit in it. Cornelius gently drops the ball into Kathryn's lap, and then when nothing happens, retrieves it and places it in Emily's lap. Kathryn and Emily watch the soccer players try to regroup, standing close together now and kicking the ball weakly to one another.

Do you want kids? Emily says.

I had thirty, Kathryn says, and she can feel Emily's eyes on her. I taught kindergarten, Kathryn says. One year's worth, anyway. I had nightmares about losing a kid.

Emily nods. She stands up, throws the ball, and sits back down. I might want one, Emily says. But then I can't imagine, and she gestures to the space where the woman had been.

There are sirens somewhere. Kathryn and Emily listen closely, trying to discern what the sirens might tell them. Help is on the way? The worst is yet to come? It sounds at first like the wails are coming closer, but then they are fading into the distance and gone.

My friend lost a baby, Kathryn says.

Kathryn had been there in the exam room when the doctor told Sharon. It was Kathryn who had asked all the questions. It was Kathryn who wrote down the procedures and dosages on a piece of paper she dug out of Sharon's purse. It was Kathryn who slept in the waiting room and yelled at people when they needed to be yelled at. It was Kathryn who tracked down Kyle at his conference and told him to come home. And it was Kathryn who got Sharon home in one piece. And it was Kathryn who made the dozens of phone calls to postpone the wedding, which had been scheduled, confidently, for a month after Sharon's due date.

Even in the months that followed, when it was less clear what could be done, Kathryn had been there every day with food and love, until men came with a moving truck and took everything away.

It sounds like you were a wonderful friend, Emily says.

And it's true. Kathryn had been a wonderful friend. She would have done anything for Sharon and she'd do it again, though at the moment Kathryn is avoiding Sharon's phone calls.

When she rescheduled the wedding, Kathryn says, she put it on my birthday.

On purpose? Emily says. Why?

Kathryn doesn't know why. All she can think of is Sharon on the floor of that exam room.

Cornelius knows the way home. He is leading them there. He is a demonstrably happy dog and Kathryn and Emily discuss what kind of animal they would most like to be. Kathryn says a cow—she has been saying cow since she was five—but then Emily says manta ray, which makes Kathryn want another turn.

They're crossing Kitchener when they see the little girl alone on the wide sidewalk. She can't be more than three. They call out to her as they approach.

Are you lost, honey? Emily says.

The child backs away, off the sidewalk and in between two parked cars. Kathryn and Emily stop. The child regards them with wet, watchful eyes.

Emily tries again: Sweetie, do you live in one of these houses?

The child says nothing.

She might not speak English, Kathryn says.

Emily gestures with one hand—big, slow scoops of air, drawing the child toward them—but the girl inches back, almost into the road.

Kathryn says, Aisha, I need everyone to be on the sidewalk right now.

The child seems to consider this.

Nobody goes home until we're all on the sidewalk, Kathryn says. Do you understand, Aisha?

The child nods.

Then whenever you're ready, Kathryn says, and sits down smartly on the sidewalk. Emily drops down beside her and pushes Cornelius's butt to the ground.

Once on the sidewalk, the child tries to disappear into Cornelius.

Kathryn and Emily ask all the questions you might ask, but Aisha says nothing. She nods yes sometimes, but never no, so it's hard to completely trust the yeses.

Do you have your phone? Kathryn asks Emily.

It's charging, Emily says. She looks guilty.

Kathryn's is shoved between the sofa cushions at home.

They ring doorbells and listen to the chimes through the door. Sometimes dogs bark from inside, but no one answers.

Should we take her back to the park? Emily says.

Kathryn doesn't think they should move her from this spot.

I'll go, Kathryn says. She says, Aisha, I'm going to go find your mommy. And you and Emily and Doggie are going to sit right here, okay?

Aisha nods, and holds one of Cornelius's floppy ears up over her face.

Kathryn runs the four blocks. Not all-out runs, but hard and fast. It feels good. She imagines what she will say to the frenzied mother, what words she will use to cut through the panic and get her to listen and come. God, it feels so good to run right now. Why does it feel so good?

The park is abandoned when Kathryn gets there. The soccer guys are gone. Kathryn stands very still and listens for the mother's far-off voice, but there is nothing to hear except her own laboured breathing. Kathryn calls out to the woman in the only way she can think—she yells the name Aisha, loud and long, until her throat is raw.

When Kathryn gets back to their little piece of sidewalk, rain is crashing down. Emily has wrapped her jacket around the girl, who is crying now.

His place is just a few blocks away, Emily says, indicating Cornelius. We could use their phone.

Kathryn looks around for some sort of cover, or pay phone, or human being in this city of one million.

Aisha, Kathryn says, do you want to come home with us?

The child cries harder.

Kathryn crouches down before her. Do you want to see Doggie's house? Kathryn says, and Aisha nods. Kathryn boosts the girl up onto her hip and stands up. This seems like a terrible idea, Kathryn says.

I know, says Emily.

And this is what we're doing? We're doing this?

Emily nods. She is shivering now.

Okay, says Kathryn. And they run.

Emily calls the police while Kathryn tries to find something dry for Aisha to wear. The child's teeth are chattering and she is whimpering, but she has cried herself out. Cornelius has put himself in his overnight crate and watches them doubtfully through the open door.

It is a thoroughly childless house. The closets are all silk and dry-cleaning bags and nothing to fit a frozen toddler. Kathryn rummages through dresser drawers and finds, at last, a thick cable-knit sweater that reaches down to Aisha's toes.

Better? Kathryn says, and Aisha nods. Or at least Kathryn thinks it's Aisha. It is slowly occurring to Kathryn that they just took this child, this child they assume is Aisha. They picked her up off the street and carried her away.

The police are on their way, Emily says.

They sit on the living room floor with Aisha and try to improvise toys out of empty Tupperware containers and napkin rings.

Aisha receives these items with some indifference, but after a while they are all three engaged in a slow, complex game, the rules of which are unclear.

Is there anything warm we can give her? Kathryn says. The girl's lips are blue. The kitchen is largely decorative, with more cookbooks than actual food, but Emily turns up a can of pumpkin from the cupboard and a can of coconut milk, and she microwaves these together with some maple syrup, which Kathryn thinks is brilliant. They all eat from the same big bowl and Aisha laughs.

Right away, the police do not like them. The first two officers scold them for not having their cell phones.

You should always have it with you, the bigger one says, like it's the law. Two more officers arrive. They are filling up the room with their guns.

Now which one of you lives here, says the one cop.

Neither of us, says Emily, I just walk the dog.

So whose house is this?

Emily doesn't know their names. Does she know how to reach them? No. Does she know where they work? No, she does not.

Do these people know you're in their house right now? he says.

Basically, says Emily.

And when we find them, they're going to confirm that?

They don't know who I am, but yes.

He writes something in his book.

And what's the relation here, he says, his pen waggling back and forth between Emily and Kathryn.

She's a friend, Emily says.

Meaning what?

We just . . . know each other.

How do you know each other?

She's dating my boyfriend, Kathryn says.

At this point, the police move them to separate rooms.

Kathryn is parked in the kitchen and made to feel she did the wrong thing. But she knows that's not true. We did the right thing, she says to the young cop who she supposes is guarding her. He looks away.

Eventually, another police car arrives with two more cops and the distraught woman from the park. Kathryn can see her through the kitchen window coming up the walk. She looks like she has been broken open and then reassembled from pieces. Kathryn hears, but does not see, Aisha running into her mother's arms.

After several minutes, the woman is brought over to take a good look at Kathryn, and then Emily, but all she says is, I do not know these people, and walks away. Kathryn can hear Emily in the next room, calling after the woman.

We saw you in the park, Emily says.

The woman and Aisha are taken away, the girl still wearing these people's sweater. The second police car leaves soon after. The house gradually empties until it is just the first two officers. Kathryn can hear their radios hissing in the living room.

Hey Emily, she calls.

Yeah?

We did the right thing.

You were great, Emily says.

Hey in there, the one cop says, but he doesn't add anything else.

Kathryn looks at the dirty dishes on the counter, the orange glop congealing on the bowl, their three spoons. She wonders if she could wash them while she waits.

Hey Emily, she says.

Yeah?

You want to get sushi after?

The police hate them.

CHAPTER 9

Ahimsa

The last time Chris saw Kathryn in this skirt, she was slow dancing with gay men. It was at Pat and Michael's wedding, late into the DJ's final set, and Chris sat with their coats, admiring her. She was amazing. He couldn't believe he got to go home with her.

The time before that, it was his sister's wedding, where Kathryn taught his step-nieces how to fold napkins into perfect white roses. He remembers easing the skirt off her later that night in the hotel room and sliding it onto a clothes hanger.

It seems a little nice, this skirt, for dinner at Emily's house, but then Chris is wearing his best sweater. It feels like an occasion.

Oh Emily, there is so much I have to say.

It's not Emily who answers the door.

I'm Kendra, says the not-Emily. She offers her hand and pulls them into the steamy house.

What Chris knows about Kendra: Scary-smart, at least about some things; can be funny; sometimes hurts Emily's feelings; mother of Zachary, age five.

Our little Emily's on the phone, Kendra says, and then she sort of grimaces. Don't worry, she says, we'll take good care of you. Kendra holds out her hand for their jackets. There are a dozen coat hooks on the wall, jammed with coats, but then there are two empty hooks, right together at the end, as if waiting for Chris and Kathryn.

Chris notices a small head peeking around the corner of the vestibule.

And who is this? Chris says. He knows it is Zachary.

What Chris knows about Zachary: Threw up an entire pumpkin pie; likes riddles; sneaks into Emily's makeup, which she keeps mainly for him now; the kind of kid who makes you want to have kids, according to Emily.

Zachary, Kendra says, can you come say hello?

Hello, says Zachary from behind the corner.

Chris says, Hey Zachary, how old do you want to be when you grow up?

Twenty, says Zachary. No, wait. A hundred. And then he starts to think on it.

Chris thought up this question last week when Emily first invited them over to dinner. I want you to meet my people, she'd said. Chris thought he would have to convince Kathryn, but Emily had already called her. They call each other sometimes now, Kathryn and Emily. Of course I'm coming, Kathryn said when Chris asked. I told you I'm going to be part of this thing.

———

Kendra gives them the tour and Zachary comes along to make sure she does it right. It's clearly a well-rehearsed number. It takes the better part of an hour.

Kathryn is full of questions about the workings of the house: How long have they lived here? Who owns the building? How did they all find each other?

But Chris is not interested in their rain barrels or their walk-in pantry of preserves. What interests Chris is which room has a phone cord running to it, stretched across the dark hallway and pinched against the door frame. What interests Chris are Emily's clothes hanging on a drying rack, the shirt she wore on their date. He can call it a date now. What interests Chris is the chore chart with Emily's name printed neatly beside UPSTAIRS BATHROOM. There's a checkbox for every week and not all of them are checked. Oh Emily, let me do your chores. I will come while your housemates sleep and every surface will shine.

The tour culminates in the kitchen where Naveed is worrying over several pots of food with a single spoon.

What Chris knows about Naveed: Father of Zachary; absorbs five newspapers every morning; leaves little notes around the house, ostensibly written by the cat, Maslow; fell asleep at the last house meeting.

I hope you like food, Naveed says.

It's my favourite, Kathryn says.

Chris watches them talk like this about what smells so good and how you make it and here try this. It's hard to imagine Kathryn being with someone else, though that is part of the deal, theoretically anyway. It feels to Chris like a sleeper clause, because Kathryn says she can't think who it would be. And Chris can't either. The only other person Chris has ever seen Kathryn with is Geoffrey, the memory of which makes him sick. Chris tries to think of who would be good enough to be with Kathryn. Someone kind and gentle and funny and serious. Maybe Harold, from *Harold and Maude*.

Is there anything I can do? Chris asks Naveed.

Brilliant, Naveed says, and steers Chris to a large pot of beets to peel and slice. The bulbs still seethe with latent heat. Chris has to keep plunging them into cold water every few seconds so as not to get burned, and still he gets burned. The skins slough off under his touch, his fingers turning a deep purply red. He cuts each bulb slowly and perfectly.

Oh Emily, I couldn't say anything until it was for sure, but now I need to say and ask everything.

For weeks, Chris and Emily have talked about everything except Chris and Emily. She calls him most days at work during his lunch break and the hour runs away without either of them mentioning this thing that might be happening between them. Even when the negotiations at home were going well, it felt disloyal to discuss them with Emily. Also, Chris was scared that if he said out loud what might be possible, what might be taking shape between him and Kathryn, that the gods would notice his happiness and turn it upside down.

But now it's decided and everything is possible. They can be almost anything they want, Chris and Emily, and what does she want them to be? He has an acute yearning for things to be defined and declared.

Dinner is ready and Emily is still on the phone. Naveed takes an old, heavy brass bell from a hook on the wall and clangs it three times.

Ten-minute warning, Naveed explains.

Chris has heard this ten-minute warning through the phone more than once.

An older woman appears from somewhere carrying flowers.

Oh good, you're here, she says to Chris and Kathryn and gives them both long hugs. This has to be Miriam.

What Chris knows about Miriam: Arrested in the nineteen-eighties for shaking a dead fish at a cop; did mushrooms on her sixtieth birthday; has had a song written about her, and several poems; works three days a week as an addictions counsellor.

Miriam suggests they all move to the living room. Chris and Kathryn are given the loveseat. Everyone sits and they ask each other getting-acquainted questions. It's like meeting your in-laws for the first time, Chris thinks, but do these people know who he is to Emily? How much does she tell them?

Oh by the way, Miriam announces, Yvonne'll be here for dinner. My girlfriend, she adds for Chris and Kathryn.

Then Kendra remembers that someone named Raditch might or might not be coming, too.

How do you live like this, Chris wonders. How can you plan a meal with people showing up without warning? Are there even that many chairs? It feels impossibly chaotic.

———

Naveed sounds the old bell again and everyone starts circling the table and sitting down in what might be their regular seats. Chris tries to divine where Emily will sit. A large bearded man emerges from the basement and seats himself at the head of the table, or one of the heads.

Moss, this is Chris and Kathryn, Kendra says. Emily's friends.

The man turns to them placidly and does a little nod with his head.

What Chris knows about Moss: Eats the whole apple, core and all; spent six months in the Arctic, or Antarctic; installed a solar water heating system on the roof, out of pocket, and single-handedly, without saying anything to anyone.

Moss, Kendra says, Kathryn here is the one who built that dish rack that Emily was telling us about.

It's impossible to tell if this makes any impression on Moss, but Kendra persists.

Could you, maybe after dinner, talk to her about it?

I imagine I could, Moss says.

Moss has a truck, Zachary says.

Zachary wants to say grace.

Can we keep it short? Naveed says.

Zachary delivers a long, free-form benediction in which he mostly talks about his day and tells God a joke he made up. Kathryn squeezes Chris's hand under the table. He's glad she's here. If she wasn't, he would want to go home and tell her about this, but it wouldn't be the same.

In the middle of this communion, Miriam's girlfriend, Yvonne, lets herself in the front door and tiptoes to her seat.

Chris wonders how the house decides who gets to have a key. Is there a meeting? Will Chris get a key?

There is still no sign of Emily.

Naveed gives everyone a quick rundown of the food—what has meat, what has wheat—and then plates are going around.

Should I go cut the phone cord? Kendra says. She makes her fingers into scissors and snips at the air.

Be kind, says Miriam. It's her brother, I think.

The room is still for a moment.

I'm sorry, says Kendra to no one in particular. I thought she was talking to someone else.

The last thing Chris had heard about Emily's brother, Stephen, is that his phone was not in service and nobody knew how to find him. Stephen disappears sometimes, for a couple days, a week maybe, but always washes up at someone's door, dehydrated and half starved. But it's been a few weeks now, months possibly, and Emily is more worried than usual. He's so smart, Emily said, he just loses the will.

Kathryn asks what everyone does for a living. The housemates are all very impressive with their socially responsible jobs, but Chris resents them for sitting here eating and laughing while Emily is up there suffering. He wants to make a plate of food for her and carry it up to her room. He wants to rub her shoulders while she listens to her sad brother and be there when he hangs up so she doesn't have to be alone with the dial tone.

———

Kathryn is asking about the name, Ahimsa, and if it's a religious thing.

The housemates are delighted by the notion that they could be taken for a religious community, but no, none of them had anything to do with the name.

If I was anything, I'd be Quaker, says Naveed.

I'm solely carbon-based, Kendra says.

Old Moss here is a mystic, someone offers.

Moss does not look up from his food.

And then Emily is there in the room, barefoot and swollen-eyed. She smiles wanly at everyone. Miriam stands and envelops her. Kendra, from where she sits, strokes Emily's back.

What's sad? Zachary wants to know.

The housemates are good to Emily, Chris can see. They let her get it out at her own pace—the call, the terrible connection, her brother running out of minutes.

I'm so sorry, you guys, Emily says, turning to Chris and Kathryn. She steps into Kathryn and the two embrace. I love your skirt, Emily says.

Then she holds Chris and says nothing for a long time.

Emily takes the seat that Chris has been mentally saving for her.

So what did I miss? Emily says.

Kendra says, Are you now or have you ever been a member of the Ahimsa Party.

We've been disavowing our religious heritage, says Naveed.

Miriam, Emily says, will you tell them about the Cult of Mariko?

Many years ago, Miriam tells them, there was a different group of people living here. Miriam is the only one left from those days. Anyway, one of the housemates back then, Mariko, found out she had breast cancer, pretty far along, but treatable, they said. When her hair started to fall out, the rest of the house decided to shave their heads too, you know, in solidarity. We did it out on the porch, one after another. It's a more common thing to do these days, Miriam says, but back then, well the neighbours must have wondered about all these bald heads coming and going, because a few weeks later, two men came by asking questions about who we were and what were our views. It was right after the sarin gas thing in Tokyo, so people were worried about cults. So we started calling the house the Cult of Mariko for a while, even after she was gone. Everyone loved Mariko.

Zachary likes the idea of everyone shaving their heads. One by one, everyone at the table covers up their hair with their hands and Zachary laughs and begs them to do it for real, until Kendra takes him upstairs to get ready for bed. I wanna be a cult, he says.

A quiet contentedness settles over the table. There's tea, still too hot to drink, and brownies Yvonne brought.

I think I was in a cult, Kathryn says. Or my mom was, when I was a kid.

Chris has never heard her call it this before. The first time Kathryn told him about it, she said it was a trailer park. And it is—he looked it up. But then you start to catch whiffs of things, like this trailer park had its own grade school, right there on the property. Its own church.

Kathryn starts to tell them about the jello. All the little kids were led into the church and handed bowls of jello. It was green, she remembers, and cubed, and the children were excited because they never got sweets. They were told to eat, and then the pastor asked if anyone knew how gelatin was made. They didn't. The pastor said they pull out the bones of baby animals and grind them into dust. You all know Bambi, the pastor said. Little Bambi? And he held up a jiggling bowlful. The kids started to cry, pushing away the half-eaten jellos, but the pastor said, No, you have to eat it all.

They made us, Kathryn says.

God, you poor thing, Miriam says.

How did you get out? Naveed asks.

And why jello? Yvonne wants to know.

Tonsillitis, Kathryn says. That was how she got out, years later.

Her doctor said Kathryn should have been miserable—a massive infection, raging fever, far from home—but it was the happiest he had ever seen her, those three days in the hospital. He started asking questions about things at home.

Six months later, I was an emancipated minor, Kathryn says.

Nobody says anything for a while. Then Kathryn raises her tea mug.

Thank God for tonsillitis, she says, and they all drink to the blessed inflammation.

They are clearing the dishes when the phone rings. Miriam answers, then sadly holds out the receiver to Emily.

Please don't leave, Emily says to Chris and Kathryn. Chris watches the bottoms of her feet run up the stairs.

Kendra comes back down from putting Zachary to bed.

It's bad news, she says. He wants Octopus's Garden again.

There is groaning and complaining among the housemates, but they carry themselves into the living room and they sing

Octopus's Garden, loud, with Naveed on acoustic guitar and Miriam playing this small accordion. Naveed isn't great—he has to hum most of the guitar solo—but they're all so into it, Chris thinks. Except for Moss, who is doing dishes.

Chris sits on the loveseat with Kathryn and watches them play. He wonders what all this sounds like to Emily upstairs, hearing these inane lyrics through one ear and who knows what through the other.

I hope she's okay, Kathryn says.

The housemates are moving on to Leonard Cohen now. So Long, Marianne. Hey, That's No Way to Say Goodbye.

Do you want to go check on her? Kathryn asks.

Chris can't decide if that's the right thing to do. Instead he says, You should play, and nods to the piano.

Naveed stops mid-verse. You play? he says.

I only know one song.

For god's sake, let's hear it, Kendra says, before this guy starts playing Pink Floyd.

Naveed strums the opening chords of Comfortably Numb.

It takes some coaxing, but in time Kathryn is at the piano playing her one song: His Eye Is on the Sparrow.

Chris has only heard her play it a couple of times. It's astounding what fingers can remember after so many years.

When Kathryn finishes the song, the housemates want to play it with her. They go through the song again and again, working on harmonies. Chris looks on from the loveseat, where Maslow the cat is circling his lap. He thinks about Kathryn learning this song note by note in that chipboard church. He thinks about

Kathryn's mom and the masking tape and the silent times and how Kathryn survived and remade herself into this person. Kathryn the Amazing, who taught herself the entire high school curriculum in ten months, who donated bone marrow to a man she'd never met, who does little dances in the kitchen to Al Green. He still can't believe he gets to go home with her.

The singers are working on the chorus when Emily pads into the room. She sits next to Chris on the loveseat.

Are you okay? he says under the melody.

She takes his hand, their fingers lacing together automatically. They sit and watch their people make music.

At the bridge, Kathryn looks back over her shoulder, and for a second, Chris wants to pull his hand away. A reflex. But Kathryn smiles at them and turns back to the piano. She's having fun.

Chris is not entirely certain that Kathryn saw their hands, but he thinks she did, he's pretty sure. And for once, it feels real, whatever this is they're doing, like something that cannot be undone. Not easily, not wholly. He looks down at Emily's hand in his, her gnawed-down nails, his beet-stained fingers.

CHAPTER 10

Bachelorette

No doubt her choice was unwise, but a choice had to be made—three hours in Sharon's car with the always neighbourly Ann-Marie already installed in the passenger seat, a map spread purposefully across her legs; or three hours in a car with Leslie and Lori, strangers to Kathryn, math teachers.

They all understood that Kathryn was supposed to go in Sharon's car and that rat-like Maura would ride with Leslie and Lori, since they all know each other. But when Leslie asked, rhetorically, So who's coming with me, Kathryn said, I can, like she was being sociable, like we're all friends here.

Super, Sharon had said, and motioned Maura over. Things have been quietly stiff between Sharon and Kathryn for most of a month. If asked, Sharon would probably say it was because Kathryn had disappeared for two weeks—didn't return calls, wouldn't acknowledge emails—and right when so much needed doing. But Kathryn suspects the real problem is that she failed to agree with Sharon on the matter of open relationships.

It's unwise, Sharon had said at the end of her lecture on the subject.

Kathryn said nothing, and then asked what she should bring to the party.

For the first however-many miles, Leslie and Lori try to include Kathryn in the conversation.

So are you excited? Lori asks, because Kathryn is the maid of honour and so should be excited. But it is hard to think much about a wedding that is still three months away. Besides, Kathryn has done all this before. She's already been three months away from this particular wedding, the first time around. She's already been through all the planning, the buildup.

Maura says you used to be a teacher, Leslie says.

Maura, the little rodent, went through teacher training with Kathryn and Sharon. They disliked Maura—her mousy keenness, her pious tattling—and they tried to avoid working in groups with her. Now Maura works at the same school as Sharon, and is apparently the kind of friend you invite to your bachelorette party.

Maura said you do something with books now. That must be exciting, Lori says.

I make the index at the back, Kathryn says.

Leslie says, My word processor has a thing that does that.

Hmm, Kathryn says.

Still, it must be fun, Lori says, getting to read all those books.

Kathryn assures them it is not.

After a while, Leslie and Lori give up on Kathryn and start to talk about school stuff. Kathryn listens to the way they talk about the kids they like and the ones they don't. They probably think Kathryn is a washout who didn't have what it took to outsmart a bunch of five-year-olds. And maybe they're right. Kathryn doesn't much care what they think. In the back seat, she is increasingly insulated from their conversation by the bad Top 40 pouring from the rear speakers. Every time a song comes on that Leslie likes, she turns the radio up another notch, and never turns it back down.

It's going on dark when they get to the cabin. Ann-Marie starts herding them around. The cabin belongs to her brother-in-law's family, so she knows where everything goes.

It's a big place, three bedrooms, and Kathryn is still deciding which bed to put her bag on when Ann-Marie pushes a glass of champagne into Kathryn's hand and shoos her into the kitchen for an announcement. Sharon is standing on a chair.

I'm sure you've all been wondering, Sharon says, why we're not having this party closer to the wedding.

No, Kathryn has not been wondering. Kathryn remembers something about people being away for the holidays, and then scheduling conflicts in January—it's the same reason the wedding had to be on her birthday, it's just a hard time of year, Sharon had said—but now Sharon is on a chair saying the real reason is that she and Kyle have decided to start *trying* again, and that after this weekend of debauchery, Sharon won't be drinking for quite a while.

Kathryn watches Ann Marie not be surprised by any of this.

So, Sharon says, what I need from you, dear friends, is to help me squeeze all my celebrating into this weekend.

Everyone is jubilant. They all exclaim and take turns hugging Sharon. No one mentions the last, lost baby. It's not that Kathryn thinks they should, but there's not even a shade of remembrance. Instead there's champagne and tequila shots.

They drink into the night. They dance to the Cure and the B-52's and Sharon and Kathryn are exceedingly cordial to each other. Sharon keeps using Kathryn's name—Kathryn, can I get you another drink; Kathryn, would you like to pick the next CD—like they've just met and she is trying to cement the connection, but also like there isn't already a connection.

By midnight, they are drunk and bickering about wedding cakes.

I took Ann-Marie to give you a break, Sharon is saying. I know you've got a lot going on.

But why go to another tasting at all, is what Kathryn can't understand. They'd already chosen a cake, the first time around. It was lemon. Sharon and Kathryn sat with the little plates and agreed the lemon was by far the best. Why choose a new one? Kathryn has been looking forward to tasting that cake again, for two years now. But Sharon, apparently, wants a new, different cake. She'd probably prefer a new, different maid of honour, too, if they were as easy to cancel as cakes.

Kathryn says none of this. She knows she is behaving like a child and so puts herself to bed. She listens to the rest of the party from under a pillow. Around two, she considers tunnelling through the mattress, through the floor, to freedom.

It sounds like you need Sharon to be a better friend, Emily had said once over sushi. Yeah, Kathryn had said. But Kathryn knew that if she were ever able to say that to Sharon, it would be in the past tense: I needed you to be a better friend.

At breakfast, Sharon offers up the Emily situation like a party favour. It's noon, but they're calling it breakfast.

I'm not letting him have an affair, Kathryn is trying to clarify, because it's not an affair, but the women are upon her, invigorated, titillated, their hangovers vaporized. They demand to hear everything.

We are trying an open relationship, Kathryn says.

So you're swingers? Maura asks. Maura truly is an idiot.

They basically hold hands, Kathryn says.

That's so much worse, says Leslie. The rest of the women agree.

But are *you* seeing someone, Ann-Marie wants to know.

I could, Kathryn says.

Oh honey, says Ann-Marie.

Soon, they have all the dirt they need to start making judgments: It's not natural. It never works. You're lying to yourself. People aren't built that way. No one can do it in the end.

After a while, Kathryn stops arguing. She sits and blinks and shrugs. But she *is* doing it in the end. It *is* working.

There are games in the afternoon. Truth or Dare. Who or Who. I Never. These are Ann-Marie's doing.

The questions are depressingly lascivious, and Kathryn can feel the women judging her whenever the topic touches on infidelity. Judged by Maura, who slept with their practicum supervisor when they were in grad school. Judged by Leslie, who talks about her husband like she doesn't even like him, and by Lori, who just told them she has a pact with her husband about which five celebrities they're each allowed to sleep with, guilt-free. These are the women who will judge her? These are the people who look at her relationship with Chris— with Chris, who every Sunday folds Kathryn's clean underwear so that her favourite pair is on top and her least favourite pair on the bottom, who still mails Kathryn handwritten love letters from his office across town because she once said, years ago, that she missed the days of finding actual mail in the mailbox—these women will look at her relationship with Chris and be embarrassed for her?

Everyone was supposed to bring trivia about Sharon and Kyle, ten questions each, but nobody told Kathryn.

Still, Kathryn could win easily. She knows the answer to every question. Of course she knows how Sharon and Kyle first met. She was there. She was there for their first fight, too. Kathryn knows their pet names and on which date they first had sex and who proposed to whom and how.

So Kathryn could win if she wanted, and she wouldn't say no to the prize right now—a four-ounce bottle of absinthe. But Kathryn doesn't want to win. She doesn't want to answer questions. Also, Sharon is lying. She is saying now that her all-time favourite song is Here Comes the Sun, but Kathryn knows it is Careless Whisper. It has been Careless Whisper as long as she's known Sharon. Why would Sharon lie about something like that?

The one good idea Ann-Marie had was cheese fondue. The actual breaking of bread does little for the group, but the bubbling cheese has healing powers. People start telling their own stories of cheating and being cheated on. Kathryn would like to point out that there is no cheating in her case, but instead she eats more cheese. The women are talking about themselves now, not her, and Kathryn is content to let them. A box of white wine is making everyone less small-minded.

They talk, in time, about polygamy, which they've seen on TV and have strong opinions about, and this strikes Kathryn as even further from the mark. But she thinks, too, that what she secretly wanted, back before Sharon and Kyle were engaged, before things got weird, was for the four of them to be married somehow. Not the way they're talking about now, where you're in each other's beds, but that promise, that explicit understanding that she and Chris and Sharon and Kyle were bound to each other, the four of them, for life.

They brought too much alcohol and Kathryn doesn't want any more of it. What she wants is carrot juice and plain brown rice. She fills an empty beer bottle with water and holds it up whenever someone tries to hand her a drink.

It's the last night, the final push. In the morning, she can go home and this will be over.

Realizing this, Kathryn begins to tidy. She starts to put the cabin back together as it is still being wrecked around her. It makes her feel that much closer to leaving.

Maura finds her in the kitchen packing the leftover food.

I just want to say, says Maura, stupid-drunk. I think you're being so brave. I mean, I could never do it.

This rankles Kathryn somehow, though Maura clearly thinks she has offered a great compliment. She is hugging Kathryn now and Kathryn is beginning to wonder if Maura has fallen asleep in her arms when she notices Sharon watching from the doorway.

Sharon says, I'll bet Chris was thrilled when you told him you'd be away all weekend.

Maura looks around, confused, and slumps out of the room.

He's not seeing her while I'm gone, Kathryn says. Kathryn had asked him not to and he had said, Of course.

And you believe that, Sharon says.

Absolutely, Kathryn believes it. She is surprised that Sharon doesn't believe, because Sharon knows Chris, knows how relentlessly scrupulous he is.

Call him, Sharon says.

Kathryn tries to smile at this, turn it into a joke.

I dare you, Sharon says.

Everyone has been daring each other all afternoon, like drunk children, but Kathryn will not be goaded. She would, in fact, love to call Chris right now because he *would* be at home and Kathryn could hear his kind voice, but she will not be told what to do. Instead, she turns to the sink and begins to pry at the burnt cheese on the bottom of the fondue pot. It's been soaking for an hour and is just starting to give. She goes at it with a wooden spoon, a scrubbie, her fingernails. And when she finally looks back, Sharon is gone.

And that's when the anger hits. Why does Sharon get to say what is wise and unwise? Because she's getting married? Because she owns a condo? Because her life is so figured out?

Here's some trivia:

Where was Kyle when Sharon had her final ultrasound?

What was he doing there?

What was the first thing he said when Kathryn reached him on the phone?

What was the second thing?

How many days did it take Kyle to get home?

How soon was he back at work?

How many nights did he sleep in front of the TV while Sharon lay alone in a bed that hurt her?

What did Kyle say to Chris in confidence?

What did Kyle mean by "reasonable"?

There. Is that ten?

In the morning, Kathryn is packed and ready before anyone else is awake. She waits on the couch in her jacket and reads *Villette*.

The sun inches up and settles in the sky. Occasionally, Kathryn hears groans and bodies turning in beds, but it could be hours before the others are fully up.

She feels clean, like the anger has burned off in the night and left nothing but clear, open space. She feels sad, too, for Sharon this morning. These people are Sharon's friends now—some random co-workers and the woman from across the hall. Shouldn't there be a childhood friend here, someone who remembers Sharon figure skating to Whitney Houston? Maybe an old dorm-mate with stories of Sharon's sexual naïveté, her giggly crush on Ani DiFranco. Kathryn is the only person here who knew Sharon when she was still figuring out how to be Sharon, and Kathryn can already feel herself being cropped out of that picture.

But at least Sharon has someone at her bachelorette party. Who would be at Kathryn's, if she and Chris ever got married? Emily, probably. Kathryn doesn't even have dumb co-workers to invite, or some busybody neighbour.

Kathryn did have friends in university, good friends, Kim and Camille and Tami, who liked her, but Geoffrey had pruned those friendships back and back until the roots were starved and dying. And Kathryn had let him do it. Kim and Tami had come to Kathryn and said, Don't you see what's happening?, and they made her see it, but Kathryn didn't know how to fix it, didn't know how to make everyone happy.

She'd had a friend, too, at the trailer park, Natalie, who'd moved there when Kathryn was fifteen. They became best friends that same day. They'd lain on their backs in the sun-scorched grass behind the electrical box and held their pee for as long as they could, and then when Kathryn said, Now, they let it go and the hot wetness bloomed out and soaked into their denim, and Kathryn said, Now we'll be friends forever.

But then they weren't friends forever, because Kathryn got away. She got herself on that Greyhound and never wrote or called or even thought about it. She did what she had to do to survive, maybe like Sharon's doing now.

DECEMBER

CHAPTER 11

This Wordless Thing

One thing Chris likes about kissing Emily is this: it's calming. When they're kissing, he doesn't wonder whether Emily likes him the way he likes her. He doesn't worry that they're just friends who might dissolve into less. When they're kissing, they are something.

He's kissing her now in a parking lot. Or she's kissing him, which is how it usually works. Chris hasn't figured out how to make it happen himself—she's constantly in motion—so he waits, like his grandma used to wait for hummingbirds, standing by her kitchen window, patient, smiling, alert.

Soon they will have to go back to the party. Just a couple more hours, Emily has promised. What Chris would like is a small empty room with just the two of them. It's almost never just the two of them. And this is the other thing he likes about kissing Emily. No one comes up and introduces themselves— another best friend, another old roommate. No one pulls Emily aside to tell her exciting news. Everyone leaves them alone when they're kissing. Sometimes people whistle or clap, which is when Chris likes them the best.

Back inside, Chris turns it on again, the part of him that does enjoy being here. These actually are remarkable people, Emily's friends. At a party last week, Chris met a lost legend of underground film, rumoured on websites to be dead, but standing there in the line for beer. They talked for an hour about a final, unfinished film and the agony of living with footage that no one will ever see.

The week before that, a man in a fedora led partygoers in twos and threes through a series of abandoned tunnels beneath the city. The man told stories that may or may not have been true, and Chris felt lucky and grateful, either way, simply to be in this world.

And then there's Emily. Watching Emily be in the world. Watching Emily be loved, hugged, and picked up off her feet. So Chris switches it on, like a neon sign that says OPEN, and when he is introduced to someone, he asks sincere questions and reveals some true version of himself and does not immediately find an excuse to slip away. When he is pulled on stage as part of an improv sketch, he goes willingly, and when someone in the audience shouts BALLERINA! and another voice, at the same moment, yells CHEWBACCA!, Chris executes a series of slow arabesques he hasn't done since he was eight years old, all while gargling and bleating and yowling like a lovesick wookiee. And he feels more alive than he can remember ever being, though he would give it all up to be alone with Emily in her room, where tonight he will sleep over for the first time.

———

Kathryn says they're going to have sex tonight, he and Emily, but they're not. Chris is fairly certain. Kathryn has been predicting this imminent sex for weeks now, since before the kissing started. Because if I start seeing someone, she says, you better know I'm going to have sex with them.

Chris has imagined having sex with Emily. Certain aspects are appealing. He does desperately want to know everything about her, not just her stories and the beautiful working of her brain, but her smells, her taste, and what she looks like everywhere. He wants also to have something with Emily that is secret and entirely theirs. And they'd be good at it, too, he can tell. But when Chris watches it play out in his mind, when he puts himself in that scene, their bodies being good to each other, he feels the cold shadow of retribution moving across the bed. Doom. The ruinous end of everything as it is.

So Chris resolves not to have sex with Emily. He wants what they have now to go on forever. Or not exactly what they have now. He wants more, but not too much. Not enough to awaken the gods.

Impossibly, the party is only gaining momentum. At midnight, while Chris and Emily are finding their coats, there are still people arriving, from where, Chris cannot imagine. He and Emily have to push against the current of them to get out the door. You're going the wrong way, someone offers, and people laugh.

They're getting a ride tonight with Paolo, whose tiny hatchback is already overflowing with bodies. Everyone insists there is room. Chris and Emily are squeezed into the front seat, with Emily on his lap. He can smell her goodness coming through the other smells in the car.

Paolo drives faster than Chris would like. The rain has started again and small droplets are wiggling their way across the windshield without wipers.

Paolo is leaving the party early, he says, because he has to be at work at five tomorrow morning. He is a veterinary assistant. Chris looks at the dashboard clock and does the math in his head. He wishes Emily had a seatbelt. He locks his arms around her, though he knows this doesn't really work in a crash.

There is some confusion about where everyone is going and the best way to get there. It makes Chris tired. He can't think at this velocity. So when the traffic congeals around them and then slows to a stop-start crawl, Chris is relieved. He has not yet noticed the lights, red and blue, red and white, flashing. He is too busy watching the taillights of the car in front of them and pressing his foot down where the brake would be.

Probably an accident, someone is saying.

When Chris sees the bicycle lying on the asphalt, bent and broken, the first thing he discerns is that it is not Kathryn's. Kathryn is at home, asleep by now. She was already in her pyjamas when Chris kissed her goodbye. And then Chris sees the cyclist, upright, intact, talking to a cop. And the driver, standing by his car, alive. Everyone is alive.

Paolo's car creeps past the wreckage and everyone is quiet. Then Emily says, Paolo, could you drop us off first? Just like that, she makes it happen. How he admires her.

The lights are on at Ahimsa. Kendra and Miriam are sitting at the kitchen table, Moss leaning against the counter. Chris has the idea that they've been waiting here all these hours to deliver some dire news, but instead they ask how was the party, who was there, was it fun. Moss has his thumb closed in a book, like he is waiting to be alone again. You get the feeling whenever Moss is in a room with people that he was there alone and then other people showed up.

Does anyone want tea? Emily says and of course some do. She puts on the kettle. She puts on bossa nova, loud enough to be heard over the creaking water, and she dances so slightly in that way she has where you can't tell which parts of her body are in motion.

How long can it take, a cup of tea? Chris is trying to pace himself, to gauge how many minutes, how many conversational turns until they are alone. Something inside him is rubbing against something else, wearing.

He sits at the table. They're talking about something now, but Chris can't tell what. He remembers a day, he must have been five or six and visiting his grandparents, when his grandfather took Chris down to the basement and showed him how to crush empty beer cans with a bench vise. He taught him how to turn the crank arms slowly, almost silently, making it last a minute or more. Grampa said, Anytime you don't want to be upstairs anymore, you can come down here. And he showed Chris where to find the empties, in giant lawn-and-leaf bags under the stairs. It would take days to crush them all.

You doing okay? Emily asks. She is beside him now at the table, her hands resting on her cup for warmth.

I think it's past my bedtime, Chris says and is then mortified that this has been spoken out loud. But I'm good, he says. Just catching my second wind.

You poor guy, Emily says. And with that face he loves, she stands, pulls him to his feet, and takes him away, their goodnights trailing behind them. He thinks about her tea, undrunk and cooling on the table as they climb the stairs to her room and he knows that it has begun. The compromises have begun.

In Emily's room, Chris does get his second wind. There is so much to see and learn. He has been imagining this place since the day she said, Hi, I'm Emily. He has pictured the room spare and minimal, like a Trappist cell, or sensual with white Christmas lights and pillows. What he has not pictured is simply her and everything about her in drifts on the floor, a stratigraphic record of her every day. It is fantastic.

Emily finds a path to the bed and tumbles in. She groans happily. She assures her bed that they will never be apart again. Chris lingers across the room in a small clearing by the door. He watches Emily luxuriating in exhaustion, surrounded by her life. He wants all this right now, and he doesn't understand how he got it. You shouldn't get everything you want, right?

Where are you, Emily says, eyes closed and smiling. Her hand reaches out into the air between them.

There's no word for this, Chris thinks, for what they're doing, this lying in bed fully clothed, and touching one another gently in slow sleepy arcs, the flat of her hand moving across his t-shirt, up his arm, along the underside of his jaw. Sometimes she half opens her eyes, and when she closes them again, they roll back slightly like she is fainting or going under.

There is no word, but Chris is trying to find a word, because he will need to characterize this for Kathryn in the morning.

She'll want to know: sex or not sex. Actually, Kathryn has delineated three categories.

☐ kissing
☐ making out
☐ sex

But surely there is another.

Emily's hand has found a bare stretch of skin where Chris's shirt has ridden up slightly. She is mapping its boundaries with her fingertips. It seems clear that Chris could touch her anywhere right now and that this moment could fork into one of two directions. But this is nice, just this, this wordless thing, with the rain drumming down outside. So he touches her cheek, her ear, her stomach.

But at the same time he thinks, What is sex even? Where does sex start and this other thing end? If Chris held Emily all night, spooned and nuzzled her like this in the clothes they walked around in, no one would say it was sex. But if they were in their underwear? If they were naked? Is some fabric really what makes the difference? The whole concept suddenly makes no sense.

They might do this all night, in or out of clothes, if not for a quiet knock at Emily's door. It's Moss, looking uncomfortable and somewhat tender, for Moss. There's someone to see you, Moss says. And behind him there's Kathryn, wrecked.

Emily is the first on her feet, pulling Kathryn into the room and into her arms. Chris is only a second behind, stunned, standing beside them now, not sure what to do with his arms or face, except to nod reassuringly to Moss, relieve him of his duty, and ease the door of Emily's room closed.

I'm so sorry, Kathryn is saying. For a while, that's all she gets out between sobs, that she is sorry.

It is obvious to Chris that someone should say, Sorry for what? What could she possibly have to be sorry about? But Emily is the one holding her and Emily doesn't ask. Emily doesn't ask and Emily doesn't say it's going to be okay or let it all out. Emily just holds her. Chris wishes he could be the one holding Kathryn and knowing just what not to say. Comforting Kathryn is normally his job. They stand there, the three of them, while the feelings come and go.

I thought I could do this, Kathryn says into Emily's shoulder and Chris thinks: You shouldn't have to do this. You *don't* have to do this. We can go home right now. But Emily keeps holding her. And when Kathryn emerges from the worst of it, Emily guides her to the edge of the bed, it's really the only place, and they sit and talk.

I don't care about the sex, Kathryn is saying. Insisting, really. Though when she hears that it hasn't happened, she seems more frustrated than indifferent. God, she says, I keep bracing myself and bracing myself.

But it's really not about the sex, Kathryn says. It's the little words you'll make up afterward to talk about it. That's what was keeping me awake—lying there in bed thinking about how you were over here coming up with your own way of talking about things. And me being on the outside of that, she says, her voice tightening up again.

They sit with that problem for a while and it feels insurmountable, the secret language of couples, until Kathryn, to Chris's surprise, begins to speak their own language out loud.

Like easy monkeys and shy gorillas, she says (two different types of Kathryn's orgasms). Oh my god, yes, Emily says, when Kathryn explains the difference. And slushy and butterful (the state of being too full—of beverage or food, respectively—to have sex). And a signal check (just foreplay, purposely to no end). And the kitchen phoenix (any unscheduled sex outside of the bedroom).

Chris feels painfully exposed by all this. But then, here are his two favourite people in the world sitting in bed and laughing, not crying, about sex. And not just sex but everything: 63 squidoo (taking turns freaking out about a problem, so there's always one person to make the other feel taken care of); torso time (blow-by-blow debriefing about each other's day, canonically while hugging); and the phrase Would you bring me a glass of ketchup? (a gentle request to have the bathroom to oneself).

And when you wake up in the morning, Kathryn says, someone asks, Must we be potatoes? And the other person says, We must be potatoes. And that means it's time to really get up.

Emily loves this. Why potatoes? she asks. But neither Chris nor Kathryn can remember why potatoes. They've been speaking this language for nine years.

They're lying down by now, the three of them, in Emily's double bed. A flickering of giddy relief is catching at Chris, a sense of having escaped something. He cannot imagine life without these two people, and here they both are, everyone alive.

I'm wondering, Emily says, should we take sex off the table?

Kathryn declaims again that it isn't about the sex, and Emily says, But maybe it is a little.

Kathryn appears to consider this. She squints up at the ceiling for what feels to Chris like a long time.

And what then, Kathryn says, you'd just be wishing you could have sex, but not doing it?

Emily says, I'm not sure Chris wishes to.

They're all three looking up at the ceiling now. Chris knows it is his turn to say something. He can feel the question pressing down on him like a weather system.

Yeah, I don't know, Chris says. He cannot at this moment picture sex with anyone. But he knows, too, that an hour ago the thought of staying in his clothes felt arbitrary and perverse. Do you? he says.

I like sex, Emily says, but I don't have to have it with everyone.

Chris wonders who would she have it with, then? With the Other Chris, who pulls into town unannounced and breaks her heart all over? The not-dead filmmaker? The guy with the tunnels? The thought of Emily having sex with other people, but not with him, never with him, makes something unexpected and alien burble up inside of Chris. He can feel himself shutting down and, to his great shame, he pretends now to be falling asleep.

He is for a long time in limbo between stupor and sleep. Kathryn and Emily talk quietly to each other and he half listens, in and out. They're not talking about him anymore, or any of this. They're talking about Emily's brother, who is back home again and doing better. They're talking about Sharon, who only calls now when she knows that Kathryn will be out, and leaves business-like messages about flowers and cutlery. They're talking about Brazil and how Emily has always wanted to go, and how she should go, but why she can't.

It'll be sunup soon, and Chris wonders what the housemates will think of him, emerging from the bedroom with two women. They'll probably think he's an asshole. He feels oppressed by the people living all over this house, above and below him.

He does not, however, in this crowded bed feel the urge to be more alone with Emily. It feels good with Kathryn here. Kathryn is not people. Kathryn and Emily have never been people and he loves them each and both. A small wave of joy is cresting over him. He might be asleep already, dreaming them and this.

CHAPTER 12

Being Potatoes

There is something about sleeping with people, really sleeping with them. It's the human version of photosynthesis, Kathryn thinks. She is not fully awake yet, but lying here between Chris and Emily's respiring bodies, this idea feels powerfully true. Like photosynthesis, there are key ingredients, a specific chain of events—the proximity of limbs anticipating sleep, then the long nothingness of it, and ultimately emerging together, full of chemical bonds and simple sugars, into a new day.

Kathryn will tell this to Chris when he wakes up, he will love this, though already she is losing hold of the details.

She cannot sense in her body how long she has slept. It is light out. The sun is flooding in through Emily's uncurtained windows, but this could mean two hours or twelve. Who knows what time they fell asleep. There is on Emily's headboard a small travel clock, but blank-faced, with the batteries sitting beside it. Emily seems to live in a world without alarm clocks.

Kathryn could slip out now before the other two wake, and the thought of this, of Chris and Emily waking up and finding her gone, is somehow appealing. It gives her power over something, but over what? What does Kathryn want power over?

There were certain nights back at the trailer park when they all slept on the floor of the church, grown-ups and kids slotted together like a giant puzzle. Kathryn had looked forward to those nights, and when everyone was settling to sleep, the whole seething floor of them, she would pray God to come in the night and lift all the trailers up and away and leave nothing but the church, so they'd have to sleep like this every night, all together. When morning came and everyone went home to their still-standing trailers, Kathryn would ask her mother when the next lock-in would be—next week? next month?—but her mother would say it was not right to wonder too much.

These are her best friends now, she realizes, Chris and Emily.

Kathryn will never tell Sharon about this night, about telling Chris to go sleep with Emily, that it was not a problem, and then going slowly berserk with jealousy. She will never tell Sharon about stalking around in the rain, crossing streets without looking, and showing up at the door of her boyfriend's girlfriend and blubbering incoherently in front of that taciturn mountain man, and being led through the dark house and up into the room where they were in bed, and then crawling into that bed between them like some little child afraid of monsters, and then talking and talking and sleeping hip to hip to hip with her tormenters and also the only people who care about her, and waking up with this notion of photosynthesis, feeling fresh and green and remade from the inside out. What she will tell Sharon, if Sharon asks, is that things are going fine. Not much to report.

Kathryn would like something to read now. She has that urge she sometimes gets in strange houses to open someone else's book, one she would never choose herself, and fall into it. But there are no books in this room, not on any visible plane. The bookshelf is full of CDs, most of which, Kathryn can see, have handwritten covers or none at all.

That man Moss had a book last night when he came to the door. Something about a bark canoe. She would like to read about bark canoes right now. Or an unsolved murder. Or the peopling of Mars.

Instead, she stirs Chris lightly with her hand on his arm. I'm gonna go, she says, without meaning to. She was hoping to say something tender.

I'll come with you, he says, and then it's the same stupid conversation all over again, with Kathryn trying to convince Chris that it's okay, that she's okay, and Chris trying to convince Kathryn that he would give this up, walk away from his own happiness, to ensure hers.

Chris, it's going to be hard sometimes, Kathryn says. You have to deal with that.

But it has never been hard for them before. For nine years, being together has always been the easiest thing to do.

———

Emily wakes up with a stretch, a yawn, a high pterodactyl shriek. Kathryn feels a small wave of adoration for Emily, and cannot tell if it is Chris's or her own.

Hey you two, Emily says. She reaches out and touches them both, just lightly touches them. Emily is puffy and creased with sleep and does not look like someone who would steal your boyfriend. She looks like a soft, guileless thing who honestly believes this can work.

Wow, I have to pee, Emily says.

Kathryn has needed to pee for some time now, but didn't want to wander the hall alone. Part of her knows, too, that once she gets out of this bed, she cannot crawl back in. This is a one-time thing, and she has used it up.

So what should we do today? Emily says. She is sitting now, her back discreetly to them, slipping on her bra under her shirt. Kathryn watches, as does Chris. It seems so matter of fact. Kathryn wishes now that she had taken her own bra off in the night.

I should probably head home, Kathryn says, again. This keeps coming out of her mouth.

Oh don't go, Emily says. There's probably breakfast downstairs. Or lunch. You should stay, she says. Stay and be a potato with us.

They all use Emily's toothbrush. Chris didn't bring his, he says, because he didn't want to be presumptuous, though they all knew that he was staying the night. It was written on the calendar beside their fridge—

CHRIS AT EMILY'S

—the words nestled right at the lowest part of the square, hugging the bottom line, significantly. Kathryn had stared at it enough. She'd had conversations with it, mostly while Chris was at work, and what she'd come to is: So it's one night a week. The other six nights of the week, Kathryn would fall asleep being held by Chris and wake up to his furnace-like warmth, and then one night a week she would let him go. She doesn't own him. And who has Kathryn become that she can't spend a night alone? Is she not a whole person? Was Jane Goodall afraid to spend a night alone? Was Dian Fossey? No, Kathryn should *insist* on a night by herself; even when this Emily thing blows over, there should be one night a week that Kathryn and Chris do not spend together, that they're not allowed to spend together. Kathryn is brushing furiously now. Chris and Emily have wandered off.

Downstairs, a nebulous breakfast is unfolding in the crowded kitchen. There are pancakes and coffee and the smell of bacon past. Everyone seems unsurprised to see Kathryn there in her slept-in clothes, except possibly Kendra, who says, Well this is very grown-up.

You can never tell with Kendra. Does she mean grown-up as a compliment? Healthy, mature? Or does she mean, I wish you wouldn't air your adult themes in front of my five-year-old.

Zachary, though, is unconcerned. He is talking avidly to Chris about tree houses, seeming to pick up mid-sentence from a previous conversation. Chris and Zachary have a lot to say to each other about rope ladders versus slat ladders, and Kathryn wants to remember the next time she is at home alone imagining Chris over here taking long, sensual baths with Emily and whispering secrets into her ear, that he is in fact, at least part of that time, talking to a little kid about tree houses.

Zach, I like your hair, Kathryn says, suddenly wanting to be part of this conversation. Zachary's head is newly shaved and downy with fuzz.

I'm in a cult, Zachary says.

Oh, says Kathryn, not sure how to proceed from here.

But I'm the only one, he says, for now.

This is a magnificent breakfast, Kathryn says. She is spooning homemade yogurt and blackberry jam onto her third pancake.

I could make more bacon, Moss says, if you want. It is the longest sentence she has heard him utter, and Kathryn understands that this outpouring is about last night. This person will never ask Kathryn if she is feeling better or allude to their uncomfortable encounter. He did not, this morning, greet her with a long, sympathetic look, or any look at all, really. But what he will do is offer to make her bacon, which he might not do for someone who had not wept at his door.

Kathryn hears Chris explaining that she is a vegetarian, was actually born a vegetarian. Which is true. Everyone was a vegetarian at the trailer park. And other than her once-a-year can of medicinal tuna, she still keeps the faith. And yet she resents Chris saying this now, despite its truth. Kathryn can eat whatever she wants. And though she does not want to eat bacon, she would like to accept what is being offered to her, this kindness, even if it is in the form of slabs of fat from some poor pig's belly.

Bacon would be fantastic, Kathryn says, and Moss is at the stove.

———

They eat and eat and the food seems to never stop.

Emily says, This feels like a day to just nap until it's time to eat again. Or go snowshoeing, she says, as if both were equally possible.

Kathryn and Chris have been talking about snowshoeing for years. All it takes, apparently, is an hour on a bus and the cost of rental, but they've never made it happen. With Emily, though, Kathryn imagines, you could say, I feel like snowshoeing, and an hour later be buckling the things to your feet, then straightening up and crunching out across the untrammelled snow.

You do remember, Kendra says, that we're doing the attic today. More a statement than a question.

Oh sure, Emily says in her easy Emily way. There's decades' worth of old stuff in the attic, Emily explains between bites, and they're supposed to go through it today and see what can be gotten rid of. It shouldn't take long, Emily says, and Kendra makes a face of some sort, but you can never tell with Kendra.

Do you want help? Kathryn asks. Because now the idea of cleaning out a crowded old attic sounds even more fun than snowshoeing. Kathryn has never lived anywhere with an attic.

Actually, if you want to be a help, Kendra says, the best thing you could do is show old Moss here how to build that famous dish rack of yours we keep hearing about.

Again, Kathryn feels both complimented and condemned.

But yes, of course you can help, says Naveed, whose job, it seems, is to soften Kendra's blows.

The attic is small and angular and packed. You can stand up only in the very middle; everywhere else you have to duck or squat. It is everything Kathryn imagined in an attic.

They each open a box and shout out what's inside. It's like Christmas. Naveed's box is full of sad old books with titles like *The Homosexual Soul* and *Where Is God in a Riot?*

Naveed reads out random sections and everyone laughs or groans. Miriam opens a box of men's clothes and holds them up against her body for everyone to appreciate. Emily claims a pair of herringbone pants, but nobody wants the polyester. Most things go back in their boxes, marked for donation or disposal, and silent Moss lugs each box down three flights of stairs and out to his truck.

Kathryn watches him come and go, his head, then shoulders, then trunk rising stoically into the merriment of the attic, then pulling some cast-off box into his arms and carrying it down, down, down through the empty house. It's a thankless job, and he has chosen it for himself, letting everyone else play. He'll never manage like this. There's only one of him and boxes are starting to pile up, so Kathryn abandons her trove of mimeographed leaflets and heads down with a box.

Mostly they pass each other on the stairs. The first couple of times, they nod to each other, mutter little things, but soon they fall into a silent rhythm. It is, Kathryn thinks, like sharing a stream with a wild animal, each of you drinking from your separate sides, unworried but aware.

Occasionally though, they converge at the rear of the truck, where they might stand for a minute and speculate about whether it's all going to fit or how many trips remain. They are both visibly sweating, despite the cold.

You know, Kathryn says, you could just come look at the dish rack sometime.

Alright, he says.

It might be easier than trying to explain, she says.

Sure, he says, and they climb the stairs again. She feels strong in her legs and arms, even after all these loads. She wonders if it's the bacon.

When the last box is dragged from the attic, everyone is exhausted and celebratory. There is talk of going out for dinner, maybe Ethiopian.

They let you eat with your hands, Zachary tells Kathryn, and he shows her, scooping up an appropriate amount of imaginary food and placing it neatly into his mouth.

Kathryn would love Ethiopian food right now. She has always wanted to go with enough people to order one of everything. But Chris is already ducking the invitation.

We should probably get home, he is saying, as if they have unfed pets waiting or a babysitter to relieve. He is peopled out, Kathryn can tell. He has that look he gets when he has been out too long and the tractor beam of home starts tugging at his limbs.

Kathryn considers for a moment going to dinner anyway, without Chris, but she can't decide if that's what she wants or if she wants it for the right reasons. It's simpler to go home and curl up on the couch together and watch an old movie, maybe rub each other's feet. That's not such a bad way to spend the night.

Emily walks them to the door and kisses them both, Chris on the lips and Kathryn on the cheek.

I promise, Kathryn says, this won't happen again.

No, says Emily, I need a different promise. She pulls a key from her pocket and places it in Kathryn's hand. Promise me you'll come anytime you want, okay?

The key is silver and newly cut. It was clearly made for Chris. And though she won't promise to use it, Kathryn slides it onto her keychain.

CHAPTER 13

Joyful, Joyful

Chris has always liked his mom. They were a team growing up—cooking dinner together, folding laundry during the movie of the week, mapping the next day's garage sales in order of tactical importance.

When his dad finally left for good, Chris and his mom had changed the locks themselves, Chris reading out the instructions as his mom disassembled and reassembled the mechanism. Together they made enormous wallcharts of everything that needed to happen—daily, weekly, monthly—and they shaded in the boxes at the end of every day and admired their progress.

His sister Claire had no part in this. Claire was older and went to parties, and Chris did most of her assigned tasks because he could not bear empty spaces on the chart.

They worried about Claire together, his mom and he, and worked hard to at least get her through high school. It was a project, and they both loved a project. When Claire did graduate, only one summer behind the rest of her class, Chris's mom bought him a ten-speed and said she couldn't be prouder of him. Chris was twelve.

After Chris moved away, it got harder to maintain this connection. They never figured out how to have a real conversation on the phone, and without a project to chew on, they had little to say. Still, they do like each other, and when Chris's mom announced that she would be coming to spend Christmas with Chris and Kathryn this year, Chris started planning projects.

He outlines these projects for his mother on the cab ride from the airport: installing a hand-held shower nozzle (Kathryn has been wanting one for years); assembling an earthquake kit (he has printed out lists from several websites detailing what to include); setting up and decorating the tree (it's new, and still in the box, and making the whole room smell like plastic. I'm sure it's perfect, his mom says); learning once and for all how to make her legendary pickled beets (they're really nothing special, his mother maintains, but they are); and lastly, time permitting, making a gingerbread house or possibly gingerbread tree house (Chris thought he'd give it to Zachary as a Christmas present).

It's more than they can do in five days, Chris knows, and he knows, too, that this is part of what appeals to his mother. She asks questions about logistics and timelines and the best way to proceed, and they sketch out a triage list there in the back seat. They're having fun. The cab driver turns up his music against their enthusiasm.

There's also someone I want you to meet, Chris says. Just puts it out there like another offering, another fun activity, but his mom is instantly suspicious. She sets the list in her lap and gets very still.

Her name is Emily, Chris says.

Okay.

She's great, he says.

Mm-hm.

This is as much as Chris had prepared. He had imagined that his mom would, at this point, start asking mom-like questions: Emily Who? What does she do? How do you know her? Chris would know how to answer questions, but isn't sure how to keep talking without them.

She's really great, he says again, and they bump over a long bridge without speaking. His mother seems suddenly interested in the scenery. Chris watches the meter flick numbers. When it reaches $20 even, he will say something to her. When it reaches $25, for sure he will say something. He reads the decal on the window outlining his rights and responsibilities as a passenger.

Anyway, he says as they pull up to the apartment, she's coming to dinner with us tonight, so you'll get a chance to meet her.

Well then, his mother says.

Kathryn is waiting for them with tea and cranberry bread, which is, Kathryn has pointed out, how Chris's mom has greeted them every Christmas for seven years. These things mean a lot to Kathryn. In her own family, Christmas was deemed a perversion.

Kathryn dear, his mother says, I am so delighted to see you, and they hug for longer than usual, Chris thinks. Will you show me around, dear, his mom asks Kathryn, grasping her arm.

Kathryn gives Mom the tour of their smallish one-bedroom apartment. Chris tags along behind.

His mother has many good things to say about the apartment—the use of space, the choice of colours, the coziness of the furniture—and these comments are all directed to Kathryn. Kathryn, I love what you've done with this corner, his mother says. You've made a lovely home, Kathryn. Like Chris had no part in making things cozy, like Chris hadn't spent two hours in the paint store choosing the perfect shade of plum with Kathryn, like Chris is not part of the team.

It dawns on Chris that he is in trouble with his mother.

Mom says she might like a nap, and they get her installed in their bedroom with minimal fussing.

We'll need to leave for dinner around six, Chris says, so shall I wake you around five? Chris never says shall, but he isn't used to being in trouble with his mother. Shall seems like something one might say.

You won't need to wake me, she says and disappears behind the door.

Does she seem weird to you? Chris asks Kathryn as they tiptoe around the apartment. But Kathryn's threshold for weird mothers is too high. Her own mother once didn't speak to her for a full week because Kathryn, age three, had drawn in a hymnal with blue crayon. Later, when Kathryn was well into puberty, her mother had confiscated her diary and, what's worse, did not burn it. Kathryn begged her to burn it in the tiny hibachi where they destroyed desirous things, but her mother kept the diary somewhere and would occasionally hurl lines from it as weapons.

So to Kathryn, Chris's mom is the perfect mom.

She's probably just tired from the trip, Kathryn says.

Chris thinks things will be easier once they get to dinner. Emily has that effect on people.

At five o'clock, Chris's mother emerges unrumpled from her nap and says she doesn't think she'll be wanting dinner. You should go on without me, she says, and retreats to the bedroom. Chris follows.

Is something wrong? Chris asks.

I'm fine, she says. She is refolding the clothes from her suitcase into neat piles. I simply don't feel the need to meet anyone new.

Because I invited someone to dinner?

Who is this girl, Chris?

She's Emily, he says. She's a friend of mine.

When have you ever introduced me to a friend?

Chris realizes this is right. He has never introduced his mother to a friend, only girlfriends. At the moment, he can't remember ever having a friend.

Chris wants to say the most honest thing he can about Emily and who she is to him, but he doesn't know what it is. They haven't exactly decided what they are. He remembers something he once heard Emily say about the Other Chris: that they were seeing each other. And as the words come out of his mouth he thinks, this is the wrong thing to say.

And what about Kathryn? says his mother, clearly upset now.

Kathryn and I decided this together.

His mom looks at him skeptically, then returns to her refolding.

Kathryn is fine with it, he says.

I doubt that very much.

Chris doesn't say it was Kathryn's idea, though he honestly could: Ask her on a date, Kathryn had said. Hurry up and have sex, she'd said. But Chris says none of these things. He would never do that to Kathryn.

Do you want me to tell Emily not to come? he says.

You do what you want, Christian.

———

PHONE CALL

THURSDAY 5:20 PM

CHRIS: Hey, is it too late to call off tonight?

EMILY: Oh no! What happened?

CHRIS: My mom's being weird.

EMILY: Do you want me to bring food over?

CHRIS: I don't think so.

EMILY: Naveed made this giant thing of stew.

CHRIS: Actually, I think we're still going to dinner, I just don't think we should have any extra people.

EMILY: Oh. [*here, a difficult pause*]

CHRIS: I don't mean extra. I mean new.

EMILY: Chris, it's fine. I'll meet her tomorrow, right? [*Emily is coming tomorrow to help decorate the tree.*]

CHRIS: Absolutely.

EMILY: Perfect then.

CHRIS: Perfect.

QUESTIONS

Is this the way he loses Emily? Is this the moment it starts to unravel? Should he call back and uncancel? Should he call back and not necessarily uncancel but tell Emily everything and ask what she would do? Why hadn't he done that in the first place? Why had he jumped to cowardice? And what *would* Emily do? If Emily were saying to her own mom, Mom, I want you to meet Chris, my _____, what would go in the blank? Friend? Boyfriend? Nothing? And what would Emily's mom say then?

———

Dinner is liverish and congealed. Chris's mom puts herself to bed as soon as they get home. It's not even eight o'clock. Chris and Kathryn pull the futon onto the living room floor.

Do you think it's bad, Chris says, me seeing Emily?

Kathryn is mashing down lumps with her foot. Bad? she says.

Immoral, Chris says.

Kathryn snorts at the word. There is real evil in this world, Chris. I don't think you kissing someone counts.

She unfurls a fitted sheet and they try to wedge the futon into it. Corners keep slopping off.

Just leave it, Kathryn says after multiple attempts.

But Chris wants to make it right for Kathryn. He doesn't give up until he has all four corners secured, though during the night three come off.

At breakfast, Chris asks for it. He and his mother have just ordered omelettes. Kathryn has absented herself, saying to

Chris's mom that she had some last-minute gift wrapping to do. To Chris, she said, You and your mom need to get this out.

So Chris asks for it. Mom, do you have thoughts about me being in a relationship with Emily?

His mother has many thoughts, lined up like missiles. She has always been proud of him, she says, and the way he treats women, so loving and gentle. But this. This two-timing. Well, for the first time in her life, she is ashamed of Chris. She does not know what she would say anymore if someone back home were to ask how her son is doing these days, and people do ask, she says.

She feels, too, that Kathryn is not okay with this, could never be okay with this, even if Chris has convinced himself that this is something they have decided together. What choice did Kathryn have, really?

Furthermore, his mother wants to assure him that she would not have come if she had known this was going on. She would have gone to spend Christmas with Claire and her squalling family, and she still might.

I never expected this sort of thing from you, Chris.

She does not explicitly compare Chris to his father, and Chris does not, for the most part, argue with her. He offers some relevant facts here and there, but mostly he listens and swallows it all down.

———

PHONE CALL

FRIDAY 11:20 AM

EMILY: Let me guess. Tree-trimming is off.
CHRIS: I'm so sorry.

EMILY: What's going on over there?

CHRIS: Oh, I'm a womanizer. And I bullied Kathryn into going along with my self-serving agenda.

EMILY: Wow.

CHRIS: Also, I'm using you for sex.

EMILY: Double wow.

CHRIS: I don't know.

EMILY: You know none of that is true.

CHRIS:

EMILY: You know Kathryn is a strong, smart, capable woman who can make her own decisions.

CHRIS:

EMILY: She's Kathryn the Amazing.

CHRIS: Yeah.

EMILY: And I assume you know that in order to be using me for sex, we'd have to be having sex.

CHRIS: Yeah.

EMILY: We're going to get through this.

CHRIS: Yeah.

QUESTIONS

What does getting through this even mean? Long-term—ten, twenty years from now—what does getting through this look like? Is he taking both Kathryn and Emily back home for Christmas, letting his mother's neighbours say what they want? Is he fifty years old and still going on dates and making out in parking lots? What are they trying to accomplish?

———

A quiet truce settles over the day. His mother has said everything she might reasonably say and Chris has borne it. There is
nothing else to discuss if Chris is not going to defend himself. So
they pull the dismembered tree from its box and lay out the
limbs by size and shape on the floor. The instructions are
missing, they discover, which is perhaps good fortune. It gives
them a problem to struggle with and unite against, mother and
child against the Christmas tree.

His mother tells the story of her childhood Christmas tree
catching fire. Trees were always catching fire back then, burning
down entire homes full of still-wrapped presents. The newspapers
made sure to emphasize the still-wrapped presents. In her own case,
their dog, Derby, a Jack Russell terrier, barked and barked until her
father ambled over with a fire extinguisher and put the blaze out
with a single white blast. The powder looked like snow on the tree.

Chris doesn't tell the story of him and Kathryn and Emily
choosing this tree together and how they'd had to portage it
across town, the box disintegrating in the sleety rain, because the
bus driver wouldn't let them on with it, and how they'd felt like
polar explorers, trudging through the slush and snow, or that
since then they've started referring to themselves as the Nimrod
Expedition whenever they do something together, the three of
them. He doesn't mention Emily at all. And by the end of the day,
there is an almost festive feeling between them, like hostage and
captor exchanging presents on their first holiday together.

That night, when they are safe in bed, Chris says to Kathryn,
Did I coerce you into this?

How would you coerce me, Chris?

I don't know, he says. He knows that Kathryn is strong and smart and capable. What he can't figure out, and what he wants to ask, is how did Geoffrey coerce her? How did Geoffrey convince the strong, smart, capable Kathryn that she deserved so little? That's what's eating into Chris.

Look, Kathryn says, there's nothing immoral here, or bad, or wrong. No one's coercing anyone. But can we try not to freak your mom out?

Sure, Chris says.

Can we just not bring it up?

Yes.

Kathryn rolls over, her spine to Chris, and then scootches back into him. He snakes his arm through her arms and around her. The plastic tree looms up over them, off-gassing into the room.

———

PHONE CALL

SATURDAY 3:45 PM

EMILY: How you holding up?

CHRIS: Still alive.

EMILY: Oh, friend.

CHRIS: I don't know if it's going to work out this time, you meeting her.

EMILY: I get that. I might actually go away for a few days.

CHRIS: Away where?

EMILY: Chris's band is in L.A. for a week.

CHRIS: [*silently hates L.A.*]

EMILY: I'd be back for New Year's, or just after.

CHRIS: Wow, that's great. Can you afford that?

EMILY: Chris said he'd buy the ticket. He's trying
          to book something right now.

CHRIS: [*The spontaneity of it bothers him. Who decides,
          on Christmas Eve practically, to fly to L.A. to see
          a band? He hates that it's L.A.*]

EMILY: I promised months ago I'd come see him on
          tour. Now seemed like a good time.

CHRIS: Makes sense.

QUESTIONS

Why does it have to be L.A.? Why couldn't the band be playing in
Guelph or Akron or Missoula? And where would she stay in L.A.?
With the band in some motel? Four guys in a room? Will there be a
little kitchenette, or will she have to eat all her meals out? Will they
sleep together? That guy on top of her, sweating and grimacing in his
Guns N' Roses t-shirt? Or do they splurge for their own room? Order
room service and smear their bodies with custard and spend the
whole day eating it off? And why shouldn't they? What right does
Chris have to wish she wouldn't? Won't he be sleeping with someone every night? Showering with someone, kissing someone, and,
if his mom weren't in the next room, conceivably having sex with
someone? Why shouldn't Emily? How is it any different, asshole?

———

Over the next few days, Chris is gradually let back in by his
mother. Together they install the hand-held shower nozzle with
just the right amount of difficulty. They find a Methodist

church in the phone book and go to the Christmas service and sing the songs they grew up singing. They make twenty pints of pickled beets while Kathryn practises piano chords on the kitchen table. They make and eat several batches of gingerbread walls until they find the right blend of edibility and load-bearing integrity. By the time his sister phones for her annual belated Merry Christmas call, Chris and his mom are a team again.

Chris doesn't hear from Emily and isn't sure if he should expect to. He calls her cell, but it is Naveed who finally answers. I thought she was in L.A. with you, Naveed says.

Chris can't stop thinking about her and the still-wrapped present he never got to give her and how it could burn up in the night, and how none of this would have happened if his mother had only said, Yes, I'd love to meet your friend.

Emily is part of my life, he says on the way to the airport. His mother acts confused, as if she doesn't know who he's talking about, but Chris presses on. If you want to miss an important part of my life, he says, that's your choice, but.

His sentence simply runs out. He had thought he had a *but*.

His mother studies her lap. She picks a fibre off her dress and lets it drop to the floor of the cab.

Then you should break up with Kathryn, she says.

I told you, Kathryn is fine.

That's baloney, Chris. Can't you see how sad she is?

She's always sad, Mom. We're both always sad.

Chris wonders how long this has been true. How long they've been trapped in this sadness together.

You're not sad, his mother says. It's called being an adult.

JANUARY

CHAPTER 14

Housecleaning

Emily came back from L.A. vomiting. Cheerful and undying, but vomiting. On the plane, in the cab, up the front steps of Ahimsa, and, for two days now, into a large Tupperware bowl beside her bed. This is how Kathryn ended up at Emily's housecleaning job with a key around her neck and a list of tasks in Emily's shaky handwriting.

Emily had called Kathryn the day before and said she hated to ask, but Kathryn was in fact glad to be asked. It was a big favour. An imposition, actually. Kathryn had her own work to do. But it felt good to be asked, and Kathryn liked the idea of her and Emily being indebted to each other, imposing on each other, back and forth, until they could come to each other with anything, big or small, because they had already tramped down the brush and brambles.

Kathryn eases the front door open, just wide enough for her head, and calls into the house. They'll already be gone by eight,

Emily had said, but Kathryn remembers something else Emily had said, months ago, about always half-expecting to find the body of Janine Marten, the unhappy mother, waiting for her. So Kathryn calls out as she enters, in a friendly sing-song. Hellooo. It's Emily's friend. Here to do the cleaning.

Kathryn checks the whole house, room by room, pausing outside each doorway to visualize what she might find inside—a body in the tub, a rope creaking under weight—and how she wants to react, not with a shriek and horror, but with compassion and solemnity.

But the house has only signs of life. Bath toys still wet and dripping. Picture books left open, mid-story. Nightlights burning steadfastly. Kathryn circles back through each room again, gauging what she can accomplish in five hours. It's invigorating.

Vacuuming is the main thing, according to Emily. The place is always so clean when I get there, she'd told Kathryn, there's not much else to do.

But as Kathryn pushes and pulls the vacuum through the house, she finds more and more that wants doing—the light switches ringed with a grey film of fingers, the base of the toilet woolly with dust, the frosted globe of a ceiling fixture dotted with the unmistakable shadows of spider carcasses.

The house is not clean, Kathryn thinks. The house is tidy, with a smothering under-layer of grime. Once Kathryn sees it, she sees it everywhere. It could pull a person under.

She works on surfaces first, then the creases and folds where surfaces meet. The kitchen counter, she can see, is routinely wiped, but the small gap where the counter meets the stove is crusted with jam and slops of sauce. You have to move things to get a deep clean. You have to wrestle the stove out from the wall and clamber behind it.

Kathryn remembers the women at the trailer park, descending on a home. It happened sometimes that a family would leave in the night. Invalids, they'd be called the next day in church, and then never spoken of again. After a week or so, the women would converge on the abandoned trailer early on a Saturday morning and scour into the night. Kathryn was brought along occasionally, once she was old enough to really work.

The women did not talk about the deep clean. They didn't sing hymns while they worked about the cleansing power of Jesus. They worked mostly in silence, with a wrathful joy, as if the affront of the task fuelled them and nourished them.

Kathryn feels some of that now. The harder she scrubs, the more energy she has for scrubbing. Whenever she discovers a new seam of muck, she feels a twinge of relish. She wishes now that she had more than five hours.

Kathryn wonders if the women convened when she left the trailer park. If they pressed themselves into her tiny bedroom and elbowed each other in their vehemence. Or if her mother had sent them away and done the thing herself, scrubbing and scrubbing until she found satisfaction.

Kathryn talks to Janine Marten as she cleans. Do you have scouring pads, Janine? Do you have someone you can talk to? Are you sleeping at night? Janine, how old is this potato salad?

Kathryn tells jokes that her students used to tell her—strange, improbable jokes—and sings songs in a loud, brassy voice she never uses. Take Me to the River. I Put a Spell on You. She tries out versions of the toast she will give at Sharon's wedding. What do you think, Janine? Too maudlin? Or just the right amount?

But also, Kathryn listens. She listens to the house settle and sigh. She listens to the quality of the silence in each room, and whether it sounds serene or lifeless. More than once, she thinks she hears a voice muttering something low and incomprehensible, but has convinced herself that this must be someone walking by outside.

The bed is already made in Janine's room, but being thorough, Kathryn pulls back the covers.

The grease is visible, a waxy discoloration where Janine lays her body down at night. She sleeps on the far side of the bed, like Kathryn, away from the door.

Kathryn pulls the sheets from the bed, and the pillowcases, heavy with the unwanted cells of Janine.

There is a hall closet, Kathryn finds, full of clean linens, and she chooses the softest ones. She puts on the sheets in silence, taking care. And when the bed is made again, she lies down on it for several minutes, so the bed does not look too taut and unforgiving. No one should come home to a bed that looks better off without you.

From this low angle, Kathryn can see the dust coating the nightstand and everything on it—medicated lip balm, seven pennies, a foam earplug. There's a calendar, small and tent-like, the kind that insurance companies send you in the mail, but it's from last year, the year that just ended, and all the days are Xed off.

Kathryn flips backwards through the months. If she could find even one date that was circled, one date with a little star drawn beside it or an exclamation point or a daub of highlighter, Kathryn could believe that the Xs had been counting down to something, marking off days in anticipation. But instead, she knows, they are simply a record of days gotten through.

It occurs to Kathryn, lying there on a stranger's bed, that she herself might be depressed. The prospect of it startles her.

She doesn't want to kill herself exactly. Like most people, Kathryn wants to be old and die in her sleep, but she wishes that it wasn't so very far off, so many days to get through and cross out.

Kathryn tries to think of one thing she is looking forward to, but the only thing on her own calendar is the unfortunate wedding blotting out her birthday. Kathryn doesn't generally celebrate her birthday, but she might've wanted to have a party this year. She hasn't had a party for how long now?

She gets out of the bed and clears the nightstand. She wipes each item, every penny, and puts them all back in place.

The energy that had flooded Kathryn has drained away, leaving her tired and woozy. There are still things she meant to do. The crisper drawers from the fridge are soaking in the sink, but the thought of getting them rinsed and dried and coaxed back into their tracks, it all feels insurmountable.

She wanders from room to room, looking for some task that would require no effort, but the house has turned against her.

She finds herself after a while on the couch watching Janine Marten's big TV. Daytime television invariably makes Kathryn angry, and she would rather feel angry right now.

She watches people losing weight on the large TV. It's a contest. They have teams and coaches. It seems, from the comfort of the couch, so doable: Basically, there's this thing you want. And in order to get this thing you want, you have to suffer and sacrifice. Specifically, you have to suffer through x-many kilowatts of sweaty effort and you have to sacrifice y-many calories of nourishment. Someone with a clipboard tells you the exact amounts. You break it down, you make a plan. So manageable, so quantifiable. But it all starts with: There's this thing you want.

What if there isn't this thing you want?

It occurs to Kathryn that not wanting things is a goal she has been working toward all her life. Now, though, she badly wants to want something. She wants to want to go somewhere, like Emily wants to go to Brazil someday, but probably never will. Kathryn could get Emily to Brazil within eighteen months, she thinks, if Emily would let Kathryn hold the clipboard. They could do it together even, suffer and sacrifice together.

But Kathryn doesn't want to go to Brazil. She could never be happy lying on a beach while poor people bring her food and drinks and other poor people are kept away. Kathryn doesn't need to see the pyramids or the Sistine Chapel or the Ganges before she dies.

The only place she can think of that calls to her is this imaginary town on a Greyhound route where she has a tiny apartment and disappears into it. She thinks about this place sometimes when she is trying to sleep. In her mind, the town is called Doppler, but it could be called something else.

The weight-loss program has ended and a home renovation show is on. She's only half watching now, flipping through magazines and catalogues on the coffee table. There's a brochure from the rec centre with all the classes being offered in the new year, and Kathryn looks at each listing to see if it is the solution to her problems. Would learning Mandarin help? Would knowing capoeira change anything?

Maybe Janine should take one of these classes, Kathryn thinks. That's what you tell depressed people: Get out there and do something, try something. Because it's easy to see what other people should do.

There are little red dots, Kathryn notices, next to each class description, as if someone has rested the tip of a pen there, considering, then lifted it and moved on. Kathryn imagines Janine Marten sitting on this couch, looking through the offerings and feeling that nothing speaks to her.

Kathryn gets that. Kathryn goes days without anything particularly speaking to her. Days when her mouth doesn't want any food in the world, and she keeps putting music on and then turning it off. And the last thing you want on those days is someone pressing you to find a hobby, or take an interest in something. Kathryn distrusts those people and their glib pastimes.

But it *would* be good to know Mandarin. Hell, Kathryn would take Mandarin. They could take it together, Janine and

Kathryn, and get coffee after and practise their greetings and leave-takings.

And capoeira. Has Janine ever *seen* capoeira? It looks so profoundly badass. Kathryn used to stumble upon street exhibitions and stand there transfixed until the dancers packed up and went away.

Kathryn roots around for the red pen and circles the Mandarin class on Mondays, Intro to Capoeira on Wednesdays, First Aid on Fridays. And when she has finished putting the refrigerator back together and folding the clean laundry and scooting the furniture back into place and emptying the mop water and taking out the reeking garbage, she leaves the class listings open and face up on the coffee table.

CHAPTER 15

Three Days

SATURDAY

It was only going to be for three days.

Emily's brother, who never asks for anything, had asked her to please come down for the long weekend, and Emily, who sometimes found it hard to go home, had asked Chris if he would come with her, for moral support if nothing else, and Chris, who was still not over Emily's last trip to California, had asked Kathryn was it okay, and Kathryn had said, Yeah, you should go, and had even talked about coming along herself before deciding that, no, she should work. That was back when they still thought it was only going to be for three days, back before anyone was in the hospital.

Emily's parents met them at the airport. Emily had wanted to take Chris for breakfast tacos at a place she knew, but her parents already had breakfast tacos waiting at home, they said. They'd gone out special and got all the makings the night before. They were so pleased about this, her parents, about knowing what their daughter would want when she stepped off the plane, though Emily herself seemed somehow aggrieved. After some fraught debate, Emily consented to just go home and eat what was there. She was quiet in the back of her parents' white Saturn. She held Chris's hand hard and stared out the window, letting Chris field most of her parents' conversational salvos.

Chris rose to the occasion, he felt. He already knew that Emily's parents were professors—her father of economics, her mother of political science—and Chris knew how to talk to professors. He asked about their respective research and listened attentively. He asked follow-up questions. He spoke thoughtfully about his honours thesis on the role of scarcity in underground cinema, and the modest ways his argument had intersected with econ and poli-sci. And in this way, he erected a shield behind which Emily could hide from her parents, who Chris secretly found delightful.

In the end, the tacos did much for morale. The Emily that Chris knew re-emerged briefly, and the four of them sat amiably enough in the bright kitchen and told stories about Emily as a small child. Chris loved this. He wanted to know every story there was to know about Emily, and he made a great audience.

They weren't going to see Stephen, her brother, until the following day, and there was the question of what to do until then. Her parents wanted to make them a big dinner, wanted to show them this Romanian film they'd gotten from the library, but Emily shrugged these off and said she might just take the car and show Chris around.

The rest of the day was all people and places. Everywhere they went, someone knew Emily. She was loved. And because Chris was with her, he was loved, too. He was hugged and slapped on the back and fed and toasted and confided in and occasionally flirted with until he fell asleep in a corner of someone's living room around midnight.

SUNDAY

They'd blocked off all of Sunday for Stephen, though no one knew what the plan was. Stephen had been staying with a friend the last couple of weeks, and his cell phone worked only sporadically. Emily seemed unperturbed by this. They spent the morning waiting-but-not-waiting for Stephen to call or text or possibly just walk in.

Emily's parents read the paper together, each with a section, reading out lines they found interesting or fallacious or emblematic of something, and then discussing the item at length. Emily dozed on the loveseat—it'd been almost four in the morning when they got to bed—and opened her eyes every so often to check on Chris, to make sure that he was still holding up and not needing to be rescued from her chattering parents. But Chris liked Emily's parents. He liked their energy—directed, as it was, mostly toward each other. He liked that they'd been in love for thirty years and still wanted to hear every single thing the other person thought about the world.

He considered phoning Kathryn. It was weird to have gone a whole day without talking to her. He felt full of things to tell her and empty of the things she might tell him. Did she finish her book? Did she order takeout from that new place? Did she find the little presents and notes he'd left hidden around the apartment? But he wouldn't call right then. He didn't want to tie up the line in case Stephen tried to call.

And then Stephen was there, ringing the doorbell.

What Chris knows about Stephen: Three years older than Emily. Taught young Emily multiplication using a box of checkers. (She had already failed the unit twice and there was talk of holding her back.) Also offered, at age six, to have his tonsils taken out so that Emily could keep hers. Got suspended from school because his book report on *Bridge to Terabithia* was judged too erudite to have been written by a sixth grader. (He couldn't produce a rough draft or outline, because he'd written the whole thing on the school bus that morning. Emily had watched him do it.) Entered university at age sixteen and dropped out in the middle of his final semester, citing tooth pain. He lived now on almost nothing, and sometimes said this was what he wanted and other times said he was ready to make a change.

He was thin and lucid and gentle, hugging first his mom, then his dad, then holding Emily long and close. He shook Chris's hand, *took* Chris's hand really, and held it still for a moment, and said, I'm glad you came, and Chris could sense the man's crushing intelligence, like the molten core of an otherwise dead planet.

They went for dim sum, the five of them, and because Chris was there, had an excuse to tell the old family stories that needed retelling. It was the first time the family had been together in one place in almost two years, and it kept feeling like something important was about to happen. But when it didn't, Stephen thanked them for coming, embraced them one by one, and headed off down Stockton on foot, leaving them to wonder what it had all been about.

He seemed good, though, Emily's mother said in the car. Upbeat. And they all agreed that that was something.

Back at the house, there were a dozen messages for Emily from friends who'd heard she was in town and wanted to see her.

What Chris wanted was to sit with Emily's parents and watch the Romanian film, and possibly drink the hot toddies they'd mentioned, and then fall asleep reading back issues of *The New Yorker* which could be found in every room of the house. For a moment, Chris considered suggesting this plan to Emily. It would be a nice gesture; parents die unexpectedly and you wish you'd spent more time. He also considered suggesting that he stay with her parents, keep them company, while Emily went out and saw her friends. He did want her parents to like him, and also he felt on the verge of breaking down at the thought of meeting one more human. But it was their last night in San Francisco—tomorrow they would go home to their manageable lives—and Chris wanted to give her everything.

MONDAY

They were packing their bags for a noon flight when the hospital called, and the hospital didn't say much. Just, Did they know a Stephen Leighby, and that they should come right away. The four of them got into the white Saturn with this information and did what they could with it.

The nurses weren't sure what had happened. Stephen had been found unconscious by an early-morning fisherman on Baker Beach. He had a head injury and was in surgery, but that's all they knew. Later that day, they would know things like subdural hematoma and intracranial pressure, but they still wouldn't know what happened. Mostly it would be a day of sitting there.

Chris did whatever he could think of for Emily and her parents. He brought them coffee. He found them new magazines when they were tired of staring at the old ones. He tried to be present when his presence was helpful and stay out of the way when it wasn't. He listened to the rational and irrational thoughts that occurred to everyone. He prayed when he was asked to pray. And he let their noon flight leave unnoticed.

By late afternoon, Stephen was out of surgery and it seemed he was not going to die. The surgeon kept saying how Stephen could've died, kept emphasizing this, which was apparently the surgeon's way of saying that Stephen was not going to die.

When they finally got to see Stephen, he was confused. He asked them several times how they got here, as if their thirty-minute drive in a white Saturn was the most notable event of the last twenty-four hours.

He would be in the hospital a while, that much was clear.

Chris calls Kathryn from Emily's dying cell phone.

Oh my god, Kathryn says. Is he going to be okay? Is Emily okay?

Are *you* okay? Chris asks Kathryn. She sounds terrible.

Kathryn has been vomiting all day, she says. Has a fever, she's pretty sure, but dropped the thermometer behind the bed before she could read it.

Chris is flooded with the need to be there, taking care of her. They always take such good care of each other.

I'm going to call right now and see when the next flight is, he says.

Kathryn says no. And he, too, had known as soon as the words came out of his mouth that he couldn't get on a plane and leave Emily with her broken-open brother. But he can't tolerate the thought of Kathryn vomiting in an empty house.

What about Sharon, Chris says. Could you call Sharon?

For what?

To bring food and stuff. To get the thermometer out from behind the bed.

It's probably just that thing Emily had, Kathryn says.

Emily's phone is beeping urgently, foretelling its demise.

Kathryn, will you please call Sharon?

If it gets bad enough, Kathryn says.

It feels now like they're arguing, and Chris tries in their last remaining seconds to change course. He loves her, he says. He's thinking about her.

The best anyone can figure is that Stephen was walking on the rocks and slipped and hit his head. It would have been dead black out there, easy to misstep.

But why was he out there at all? Emily's mom keeps saying. Isn't the beach closed at night? She can't stop asking in various ways if the whole thing with the dim sum and Emily being asked to come down was to say goodbye.

You don't try to kill yourself by tripping and falling down, Emily's father says. He is adamant about this. A bit later he says, People who want to commit suicide jump *off* the damn bridge, they don't hit their head on a rock underneath it.

Emily says little. She seems sunken and menacing, like a two-hundred-pound mine floating just below the waves. Occasionally she surfaces to tell her parents to stop speculating, stop hypothesizing, stop talking.

Privately, though, in bed that night, Emily worries that Stephen might well have been saying goodbye, whether he knew it or not. She says she had felt something like this coming since she and Stephen were teenagers, but thought it was their secret to keep. Chris massages Emily's back late into the night, digging his thumbs hard into her muscles the way she has taught him, until she at last sleeps. Then he crawls into the sleeping bag on the floor beside the narrow bed of her childhood.

TUESDAY

The second day at the hospital feels longer than the first. Chris calls Kathryn whenever there is downtime, and there is a lot of downtime. Her phone rings and rings and goes to voicemail.

Hey little bug, he says. I'm guessing your ringer's off. Hope that means you're sleeping lots. I'll try again later.

They're able to see Stephen, off and on. He speaks clearly and in full sentences, though it's hard at times to tell how the ideas fit together. And people have to explain things to him several times, like what the buttons on his bed do. Emily is the best at this, at finding new ways to explain things to Stephen and making it sound like it's the first time.

You two always did have this way, her mom says, which plainly irks Emily. But they do have this way. Chris feels honoured to get to witness it. Then he lures Emily's parents out of the room.

WEDNESDAY

By Wednesday, Chris is worried.

True, Kathryn doesn't always remember to turn her ringer back on, but it's been a day and a half. She would have checked her messages.

Chris calls Sharon at work, catches her on her lunch break. No, she says, she hasn't heard from Kathryn in weeks.

Can you go by and check on her? he asks.

Where are *you*? Sharon wants to know.

He has to tell her that he is in San Francisco with Emily and so can't go himself to make sure Kathryn is not dying alone in their apartment.

Honestly, Chris, what the fuck?

I just want to make sure she's okay, Chris says.

Are you in love with this girl?

This isn't about that, Chris says.

But Sharon says, No, it kind of is. Are you in love with her?

I'm in love with Kathryn. And with Emily.

You can't be, Sharon says. That's not how it works.

Chris exhales into the phone.

Look, Sharon says, it's possible you love both of them. I would believe that you still love Kathryn. But you're not *in* love with her.

This little word, *in*, makes Chris wild. It has never made sense to him, this love-but-not-in-love thing that people have been saying his whole life, like it's a fact we all agree on, like it's the difference between a liquid and a solid and a gas and no one has ever heard of plasma. He can feel a rage burbling up, fury that feels like it belongs to someone else, and when it reaches his throat he opens his mouth and says, Sharon, I'm going to think very seriously about everything you've said. Will you please check on Kathryn.

Chris does think about what Sharon said. She'd said it badly and much of it was wrong-headed, but she was right about one thing.

He shouldn't be here. He should be at home taking care of Kathryn. And yes, he should also be here for Emily, but Emily has her family and an entire hospital staff, and Kathryn has no one. Chris is her person and he should be there.

Sharon calls from the apartment to say Kathryn's not there.

Where did she go? Chris wonders.

Sharon says how should she know, like this is a dumb question.

But Chris can always tell where Kathryn's gone, just by looking at how she left the place. Did she take one canvas bag or two? (That's produce versus staples.) Did she wear her blue shoes? (She's gone for a walk, an hour at least.) Did she wear her blue shoes but leave the orthotics behind? (That's going to the corner store for tortilla chips.)

What does it look like there? he says. What do you see?

It smells like vomit, Sharon says.

Is there a note on the fridge maybe?

There is no note. There is no takeout or takeout receipt. There is no thermometer behind the bed. Sharon does find Kathryn's phone, almost drained, but there are no outgoing calls since last week, and the last fifty incoming calls are from Chris.

Goddammit, Chris says. He doesn't know what to do.

This is why people pick one person to be with, Sharon says.

Chris thinks Sharon is probably right.

CHAPTER 16

Ten Days

MONDAY

Chris calls Kathryn from Emily's dying cell phone. He's at the hospital, he says, in San Francisco. Kathryn is confused for a moment. She had been expecting him to walk in the door any minute now and find her like this, clammy and wretched on the couch with a trash can full of puke. She had been waiting for Chris to come make it better, or if he couldn't make it better, then to bear witness to how bad it was, which would somehow make it better.

But now it's all pouring out of him—the call from the hospital, the quiet terror of the drive, the waiting and waiting, and then seeing Stephen so scrambled, and not knowing if it was an accident, and everyone silently blaming everyone and themselves.

Kathryn almost doesn't tell Chris about being sick. Her own symptoms are hastily receding in the face of actual life-or-death trauma. It's a flu, she thinks. Probably just that thing Emily had. It won't kill her.

But Kathryn does tell Chris, because he asks, because he knows her too well.

His torment is palpable, and gratifying. He wants more than anything to be here for Kathryn. He wants to come home on the next flight. She can feel him trying to climb through the phone.

Kathryn won't let him come home, of course. It's not the right thing to do, but she likes knowing that if she said, Come home, he would.

He loves her, he says. He's thinking about her.

When the phone dies, the nausea comes back.

TUESDAY

On Tuesday, Kathryn wakes up needing to pee worse than usual. No doubt from all the clear fluids she's been trying to force down, but maybe it worked. She feels not bad, she thinks, getting out of bed. Then she falls over. She laughs at herself, stands up, and falls over again.

A wave of nausea rolls in. Her bladder cramps. She'll have to crawl to the bathroom. She gets on all fours, and still she falls over. Topples over, she thinks. Each time toppling to the left while the room, she notices now, keeps lurching to the right.

She drags herself to the bathroom, slowly, hugging the floor, but when she gets there, she can't balance on the toilet seat long enough to pee. She keeps listing over to one side and onto the linoleum.

Finally, she curls herself into the bathtub and lies there in a ball while the urine finds its way to the drain.

———

Kathryn is scared about her brain. She isn't sure what would make someone suddenly unable to walk, or even crawl or sit upright, but it seems like it would have to be something bad. Is it getting worse every minute she lies here doing nothing? Is there some mnemonic everyone is supposed to know about how critical the first few hours are? The first few minutes?

Or it could be nothing. She'd call an ambulance and the paramedics would get mad at her for wasting their time with a dizzy spell. At the trailer park, you never called 911, not for anything. You took the person to town in the pastor's old Plymouth, or not at all.

It's probably mid-morning when Kathryn's phone starts to ring somewhere in the apartment. She listens to it from the bathtub, ringing and ringing. It sounds far away, wherever it is.

It's Chris calling, she's sure. He said he'd call and check on her, and so of course he does, though Kathryn wishes for once in his life he had said one thing and done another. She wishes Chris had ignored what she'd said on the phone and instead gone straight to the airport, and that the sound she was hearing right now was his key in the front door.

She keeps catching herself expecting this to happen.

By noon, Kathryn has figured out a trick. If she lies on her right side, ear to the ground, the nausea and spinning mostly die down. She might be able to inch around the apartment in this position, if she keeps her head flat and takes lots of breaks. What would she need to get through the day? Water bottle, phone, blanket, book. Four trips, tops, and she could set up camp in the bathroom indefinitely.

She hauls herself out of the bathtub and onto the floor. She'll get through this. She's gotten through worse.

Kathryn is on her fourth and final trip, dragging a blanket behind her, when someone knocks on the door. We're not home, Kathryn thinks. She's halfway to the bathroom; there's no way she's going back to answer the door.

The person knocks again, then jiggles the doorknob. Kathryn freezes. Who would jiggle the doorknob? She can't remember if the deadbolt is on.

The person knocks again.

Kathryn pulls the blanket around herself and lurches to her feet. She makes it a couple of steps before she falls. Then up again and a couple more. She gets within shouting distance of the door on the third go.

Who the fuck is it, she yells.

It's Moss, Moss says.

Kathryn had arranged with Moss that he would come by today to finally look at the dish rack. They'd already postponed three times—twice it had been Moss who begged off—and Kathryn had ceased to think of the appointment as a real thing that would eventually happen.

Kathryn yells out where the spare key is hidden and Moss lets himself in. He pauses when he sees her on the floor, half-naked and clutching a blanket.

We said one thirty, right?

I'm sick, Kathryn says.

Moss kneels down on the floor beside her. He looks at her carefully. She can feel him taking in her hair, her eyes, her rug-burned face.

You can't stand up? Moss says.

Kathryn shakes her head slightly. She's trying to keep her right ear perfectly flat to the ground.

Fever?

Maybe, she says, and tells him about the thermometer. He stands up and disappears from view. Kathryn can hear her bed being lifted up and away from the wall, and a moment later set back in place. There's an interval of silence, while Moss is presumably reading the thermometer, then he whistles appreciatively.

Kathryn hears him running the bathroom tap.

I like your bivouac, he calls out. Kathryn hates that anyone would see all that, her underwear drying on the bathtub faucet, the spattered toilet bowl, the mess left behind. But when Moss comes back into the living room, Kathryn suspects that he really meant it, that he admires her crawling into the tub and doing what she had to.

He hands her the thermometer. Let's see what you got, he says.

Her temperature barely registers on the thermometer, but then it has been at least forty-eight hours since she ate anything.

What say I take you to the hospital? Moss says.

I'm fine here, she says.

Moss appears to consider this.

I don't need to be rescued, Kathryn says, though why she should say such a thing is not clear to her. A couple of hours ago, she was longing for precisely that.

It'd be a waste of time, she says. I'd sit there all day and then they'd tell me to go home and rest.

That's possible, Moss says.

Of course, Kathryn thinks, it's also possible they could do something for her. They might give her some pill and then miraculously she'd be able to stand up again, or they might say, It's a good thing you came when you did. But more likely, they'd say go home and rest.

And how would we even get there? Kathryn says. I can barely move without throwing up.

I could carry you, Moss says. My truck's right out front.

The thought of it makes Kathryn sick.

The ride is awful. Every time the truck turns a corner, Kathryn retches and heaves, but nothing will come up. By the time Moss carries her into the waiting room, Kathryn is sobbing and grasping for the floor.

They are rushed into an exam room. People shine lights into Kathryn's ears. They hit her with little hammers. They make her lie purposely on the wrong side, the left side, for ninety sickening seconds, make her hang her head backwards over the edge of the exam table. Moss stands in the corner and glares at them.

They gradually rule out a lot of scary things. They say, Well, it isn't this and it isn't that, and Kathryn gives them a thumbs-up and holds on to the reeling exam table. In the end what they write down is vestibular neuritis, which sounds scary but apparently isn't. Her inner ear is somehow irritated. They don't know why. Also she's dehydrated. They give her this stuff to drink and she has to take one tiny sip every minute for four hours. Moss disappears for some of this time and returns with a bendy straw so she can drink without lifting her ear off the table.

They give her a shot which tamps down the nausea but leaves the walls slowly revolving. It also makes her doze off between sips. Moss watches the second hand on the wall clock and says, Drink. Again. Again. Again.

When they finally leave the hospital, Kathryn walks out on her own legs, and Moss steers her around poles and parked cars. She curls up on the front seat and falls asleep before they are out of the parking lot.

WEDNESDAY

When Kathryn wakes up, the sun is rising and the truck is parked in front of Ahimsa. Moss has a book resting on the steering wheel.

What's happening? Kathryn says.

I thought I'd let you sleep.

I can sleep at home, she says.

I know, he says. Or you could stay in our guest room.

Kathryn rouses herself, sits up for a moment, then lies back down.

I have to pee, she says.

Moss closes his book and slides it under the seat. He looks at her like he is waiting for something and can wait a long time.

It's cold, Kathryn says.

Should I take you home?

Maybe not.

In the end, Kathryn stays in Moss's room, which is closer to the bathroom, and it's Moss who sleeps in the guest room. All they do for most of that first day is sleep. And when they wake up, Kathryn has become an eating thing.

Miriam brings Kathryn the rest of the shepherd's pie from dinner, and when Kathryn has gone through that, Moss orders Thai food, and they lie on his bed and eat. Kathryn names all the things she would like to eat right now: huevos rancheros, stuffed grape leaves, English muffins, mayonnaise. Moss says, I can go get that stuff, and Kathryn says, No, no, I don't need it, it's just what my mouth wants.

Kendra loans Kathryn pyjamas, some clean socks and underwear. Us girls gotta stick together, Kendra says, and Kathryn isn't sure what that means.

I should call Chris, Kathryn realizes. The phone doesn't reach to Moss's room, so he installs a phone jack by the bed. It takes him ten minutes. Why do you know how to do that? Kathryn asks, and Moss says he is sometimes an electrician.

Chris is distraught on the phone, crazed with worry. I didn't know where you were, he says, and when Kathryn says she is okay, that he can stop worrying, he weeps.

He tells Kathryn about calling Sharon, about calling the police, about calling his mom, about not knowing who else to call.

Kathryn tells him about falling off the toilet, about hearing all his calls and wishing she could answer, about dragging herself across the apartment.

Chris says, I'm so sorry, Kathryn. That's awful. I'm so, so sorry.

And Kathryn says, No, you should've seen me. I was unstoppable. What was the word Moss used? Formidable. She was formidable.

THURSDAY

Kathryn is bored and restless. Not well enough to get out of bed, but well enough to want to. She thinks maybe she'd like to start running, be a person who runs. Her body craves some kind of impact.

Moss's room is full of books that Kathryn would like to read, but the words keep drifting off the page. TV is dizzying and dull.

Moss keeps her company, in his way. The man cannot tell a story. Kathryn has to pry everything out of him, one bit at a time, like a pomegranate.

It's rewarding, though. He's an interesting weirdo, and the day slides by.

FRIDAY

Chris calls every day, full of concern and little stories for Kathryn. He'll be flying home on Monday, he says, now that Stephen is out of the hospital. Emily will stay another week or two, just to be sure.

I can't wait to see you, he says. He sounds tired. We'll get you back home, back in your own bed, he says.

———

Moss shows Kathryn a pair of shoes he's making. They're horrendous.

Do you know they sell shoes? Kathryn says. Pre-made.

I wanted to know how it's done, Moss says.

This makes sudden sense to Kathryn. Of course we should know how to make our own shoes.

But why just shoes? Kathryn says. Why not shirts and pants?

I did make this shirt, Moss says. He shows her the stitching, precise and peculiar.

And the pants?

I found the pants, he says.

SATURDAY

A bunch of things happen, one after another. Kathryn stands up and moves around without help. Kathryn takes a shower. Kathryn uses all the hot water. Kathryn sits at the dinner table like a human and talks to people about their day and what happened in the world. Zachary sings Kathryn a song he knows about throwing up. Moss and Kathryn order second dinner, Lebanese tonight, and sit on his bed and eat and watch some cop show on his old portable TV. And when Moss stands up and says, like he does every night, I'll let you sleep, Kathryn says, You should stay.

SUNDAY

What Kathryn likes about having sex with Moss is everything about having sex with Moss. What Kathryn likes about having sex with Moss is Moss lifting her off the mattress and then pressing her down into it. What Kathryn likes about having sex with Moss is simple yes/no questions. What Kathryn likes about having sex with Moss is him watching her, never taking his eyes off her, like she might do anything. What Kathryn likes about having sex with Moss is the angles. What Kathryn likes about having sex with Moss is the ache of her muscles, the loss of vision and speech, that feeling of drowning. What Kathryn likes about having sex with Moss is that it occurs to Moss.

CHAPTER 17

Feelings

CONFUSED

Confused at first, when Kathryn is there waiting for him at baggage claim, smiling and jumpy-eyed, saying she has slept with someone. Confused that it is Moss—weird, silent, brooding Moss—that she has slept with, is sleeping with. Confused about the timeline. Confused about how it's possible that Chris could've phoned every day, spoken to Kathryn every single day, and yet somehow there wasn't time between Kathryn realizing she might like to sleep with Moss, and Kathryn actually sleeping with Moss, to say to Chris, Hey, I might want to sleep with Moss.

JEALOUS

He does catch glimpses of jealousy. He sees its tail slithering around corners. When Kathryn tells him the whole story— they're home by this point, in bed, still dressed, and holding each other—there are moments in the telling when Chris knows that they are not alone in the room, that two people are never alone in a room, that there is always some other thing there with them, ugly and pitiless and waiting.

NOT JEALOUS

It surprises him how not jealous he is. Once he is sure that he has heard everything Kathryn has to tell, once he no longer has to steel himself for what might be coming, it turns out Chris is fine with everything.

Kathryn is suspicious of this. She pokes at it. First because she doesn't believe him and later because what does it mean that he isn't jealous? Isn't he scared of losing her? She had been scared of losing him.

But Chris isn't scared, not right now. Should I be? he asks, which exasperates Kathryn.

THE OPPOSITE OF JEALOUS

That's what it is. It isn't the absence of jealousy, it's the opposite of jealousy. It's some kind of joy. Because Chris can't remember the last time he saw Kathryn this excited about anything. He can't remember the last time she told him a story in such detail and with so many tangents and footnotes and curlicues. There is something bouncing around inside her and it's making something inside Chris bounce around, too.

I don't get that, Kathryn says.

It's like falling in love sideways, he says.

RELIEVED

He wants everyone to know. Kathryn is already asleep beside him, but he wants her to wake up and tell everyone right now. He wants Sharon to know that it is Kathryn who can't keep it in her pants, not him, so ha! He wants his mom to hear the way Kathryn talks about Moss, to hear how giddy and almost stupid with happiness she is. He wants Cynthia Welland to wake up somewhere in the middle of the night and know that Chris is not an asshole. No one is an asshole for falling in love.

WEIRD

It's weird to wake up to Kathryn writing in her journal, weird that she doesn't put it down when Chris snuggles up against her. He hasn't seen her touch this journal in years. It's weird that when Chris gets out of bed, the heat is already on. Kathryn normally makes him get up and do that, will beg and cajole, but this morning it feels like it's been on for hours. The apartment is uncommonly warm, as if the world has shifted on its axis.

WEIRD

It's weird to call Emily in San Francisco and tell her the news and have her not find it weird at all. Emily finds it sweet and delightful and wants him to put Kathryn on the line. It's weird to hand over the phone and not get it back.

WEIRD

It's weird to go to dinner with Kathryn and Moss because Moss is weird. Chris had only imagined Kathryn with someone like himself, someone he could relate to, connect with. You can't connect with Moss. He's like a mountain.

Kathryn says he's not always like that, that he opens up when it's just the two of them, that he giggles. Knowing that only makes it worse.

SWEET

It is kind of sweet, the way Moss watches her. The way he empties his water glass into hers when hers runs out. The way he blushes behind his beard when she teases him. The way he shakes both their hands at the end of the night, awkwardly, sincerely. He is a good guy, just weird.

OKAY

Yeah, it's mostly okay the first time Kathryn stays over at Moss's. Chris reads two hundred pages of a book he's been meaning to get to and falls asleep at nine. And when Kathryn calls the next morning and says Moss made breakfast and does Chris want to come over, that's okay too.

Chris wonders as he walks up the steps of Ahimsa why it should be so okay. He wasn't this okay when Emily was in Los Angeles. But he never worries that Kathryn will disappear on him. Because he and Kathryn are a team.

FEBRUARY

CHAPTER 18

The Wedding

Sharon is mad at Kathryn, maybe for the last time. The ceremony starts in forty-five minutes and they are both counting down the hours left in this friendship.

Kathryn honestly wasn't trying to make Sharon mad. In fact, Kathryn had spent weeks preparing to be the good best friend, building up love in her heart, deliberately, methodically, piece by piece, like a ship in a bottle. But Sharon is pissed.

The supposedly horrible thing Kathryn has done is bring a date to the wedding. Specifically, she brought Moss. She also brought Emily, though Kathryn is content to let Sharon believe that it was Chris who invited Emily. Sharon is mad about that, too. Kathryn isn't sure what the big deal is.

Because it's a fucking wedding, Sharon says, though this does not clarify anything for Kathryn. People do bring dates to weddings, Kathryn thinks. It said so right on her invitation.

But how does it look, Sharon says, what does it say, when my maid of honour parades in with her entire free-love harem?

This strikes Kathryn as funny, the parading. In reality, Moss and Emily and Chris will sit quietly in a room of two hundred people and eat lasagna.

No one even knows, says Kathryn, about all that.

They know, Sharon says, and she gestures to the other brides-maids—Maura and Leslie and Lori and Ann-Marie—who are pretending to be occupied on the other side of the room. Occasionally, Ann-Marie sidles over with a bottle of Chardonnay and waves it over Sharon and Kathryn's glasses, but neither Sharon nor Kathryn have touched their wine. Kathryn wonders if Sharon is pregnant already. Kathryn herself has vowed not to drink until her official duties are over, because she's trying to be good.

Sharon is saying something now about Kathryn rubbing people's faces in it, but Kathryn is finding it hard to follow the argument. She keeps leaving her body.

Five years from now, Sharon will have friends that go with her cream carpets, and Kathryn will be a hilarious story that Sharon tells about her wedding—the thoughtless best friend who decided to stage some kind of sex orgy in the middle of Sharon's special day.

Sharon will tell this story not too often, but often enough that her friends will have favourite lines and will, as these lines approach, make a show of biting their fingers in anticipation or covering their eyes.

Kathryn could tell her own version, certainly, in which it is Sharon who is the bad friend and Kathryn the long-suffering hero. She wouldn't have to embellish a thing. But Kathryn will never tell this story to anyone, because no matter how blameless Kathryn made herself in the telling, no matter how insufferable

Sharon was shown to be, in the end it would still be the story of Kathryn being thrown away by her best friend. Anyone listening to the story would know that Kathryn had had a best friend once, and had been judged not worth holding on to. And the person listening would never be able to forget that about Kathryn. She'd be forever tainted in their eyes. So Kathryn won't tell.

You just don't invite extra people to someone else's wedding, Sharon is concluding. And Kathryn gets that. She is ready to apologize for that. In Kathryn's mind, though, she wasn't inviting Moss and Emily to Sharon's wedding, she was inviting them to her own birthday. She wanted, on this day, to be with people who love her. Kathryn doesn't include this detail in her apology. She doesn't want to rub it in Sharon's face. Also, she wants to see if Sharon will remember on her own. There are still ten hours until midnight.

The ceremony is long and strangely religious. Jesus comes up a lot; more than you might expect from a justice of the peace. Kathryn can't tell if this is something Sharon and Kyle agreed to, or if it is being sprung on them. Kathryn has never heard either Sharon or Kyle mention Jesus, but you never know what couples talk about when you're not there.

Kathryn sneaks occasional glances to where Chris and Moss and Emily are standing. Chris and Emily are holding hands, and admittedly, Kathryn could do without that right now, but it fortifies her to see the three of them there, her people. Moss looks like a tree whose roots go down for a mile. Emily waves, discreetly, with her free hand.

———

The vows that Sharon and Kyle have written are vague and unactionable. I will love you forever. I will always be there for you. Kathryn isn't sure what forever means in Sharon's mouth.

Sharon and Kathryn used to make these agreements. Sharon would say, Promise when we're old ladies in the nursing home, we'll still listen to Love Cats at least once a day. Or, Promise me if my hair falls out when I'm ninety, that we'll both get fun wigs so I don't have to be the only one. Kathryn had agreed to wear fun wigs and to never learn to crochet, and in doing so thought they had agreed to much more.

After the vows, there are photos to be taken. Kathryn is sometimes in the picture, other times not. She stands where she is told, while the hired photographer shuffles people in and out of the frame.

Moss and Chris and Emily have been herded off to the reception and probably have wine. Kathryn would like to hold a glass of wine, even if she couldn't drink it. Holding it would give her a sense of purpose.

From the sidelines, Kathryn watches people pose. She watches Sharon, in one shot, rest her hand briefly on her stomach, and Kathryn knows that five years from now Sharon will sit on the floor with her little girl and say, You were inside me at Mommy and Daddy's wedding, hiding in my belly, and nobody knew you were there but me, not even Daddy.

And when the child puts a jammy finger on Kathryn's face and asks who is Mommy hugging, Sharon will say, Oh, you don't know her (though Kathryn realizes that kids don't really ask about people in old photos, because kids don't care).

Kathryn is called forward to pose with the best man. There is this obsession at weddings with symmetry, with pairing, like they all are boarding an ark. The best man is Kyle's older brother, Carl, just in from Ottawa.

We've got to stop meeting like this, Carl says.

Kathryn only met him an hour ago when he walked her down the aisle, and already he wants out.

The bridal party has to eat on stage, in front of everybody, like a chorus line. It makes each mouthful a performance.

Every few minutes, some keener in the crowd will tap tap tap their flatware against a wine glass, and then other people will join in, until Sharon and Kyle have to stop eating and kiss. People whoop and clap approvingly. Kathryn watches one man instigate this three separate times. He can't get enough, this guy.

From the stage, Kathryn can see Chris and Emily and Moss sitting at a table in the back where the seating is not assigned. Back there, they are still waiting to be called to the buffet. Emily appears to be telling a story with her hands. Kathryn leans forward. She would like to hear that story.

Is that the girl? says Maura, beside her. Maura is the only bridesmaid who is still speaking to Kathryn, for better or for worse.

It must be so hard, Maura goes on. I could never do it.

Yes, you've said that, Kathryn says. It annoys Kathryn that

this near stranger keeps volunteering her own inability, like it is a point of pride.

I just couldn't is all.

Could you drink your own urine? Kathryn says.

Maura looks at her with concern.

If you were dying of thirst, Kathryn says, alone on a life raft, would you drink your own pee to survive?

Is that what you're supposed to do? Maura says.

But Kathryn isn't sure it's what you're supposed to do.

What Kathryn would like is to stand up and walk away. And then she does. She scoots back her chair, places her napkin carefully on the seat, and steps away, discreetly, purposefully, as if there were some bridesmaidenly duty that required her attention elsewhere.

Her people receive her with quiet cheering and hugs. Chris and Emily and Moss. They have all taken to calling her Kathryn the Amazing. They are all not drinking.

We drink when you drink, Emily says, and Chris hitches up the tablecloth and shows Kathryn the four bottles of wine they have secreted away.

When their table is finally called to the buffet, Kathryn is left behind. She watches the three of them make their way through the line, choosing, discussing, considering. She has never felt this much love at a wedding.

Kathryn is struck by a sudden urge to make vows. What promises could she make to these three people right now?

All she can come up with is I will love you forever, which is barely a promise at all.

Moss brings back enough food for two, and extra cutlery. Kathryn didn't know how hungry she was until he handed her a fork. The food on stage was prop food, ineffectual like a rubber knife or breakaway bottle.

They take turns telling stories about the worst wedding they've ever been to. One had a fist fight.

Worst one I've been to was mine, Moss says, and they spend twenty minutes trying to get that out of him.

Kathryn keeps glancing up at the head table and her empty chair. They're still eating up there, making slow progress with the incessant clinking of glasses and Sharon and Kyle having to stop what they're doing and kiss like gladiators.

I should probably get back up there, Kathryn says. She's already been gone too long. Some internal alarm clock is going off in her stomach.

Oh, wait until Chris gets back, Emily says. Chris has disappeared somewhere. Kathryn looks again at the head table, trying to discern whether Sharon has even noticed her absence. Maybe it's true about your wedding day, that you're barely there at all, circuits overloaded, unable to take in anything.

When Chris comes back, he is carrying a cake and the cake says Happy Birthday. How they got a cake here, Kathryn does not know. The four of them rode here together, smashed into the cab of Moss's pickup truck. It was a two-hour drive, and there was no cake.

It's carrot cake, too, which is the best cake, and with cream cheese frosting. Now Chris and Emily and Moss are whisper-singing Happy Birthday, and then the neighbouring table joins in, and by the time they get to the dear Kathryn part, half the room is singing and craning around to see who to fit into the blank. There's applause, and someone starts clinking their glass, and then others clink along.

Kathryn feels the soft press of four hundred eyeballs. She's supposed to kiss someone.

The clinking grows louder, more insistent, like a thousand glass bells about to break. She's supposed to kiss someone, so she kisses Chris and Moss and Emily, each once on the cheek, and the room explodes with glee.

This probably counts as rubbing it in people's faces, Kathryn thinks.

A microphone appears on the stage and is tapped and blown into. The best man, Carl, will give the first toast, then Kathryn, and after that Kathryn has no idea. Her duties end the moment she raises that glass.

Carl's toast begins before Kyle is born and takes its time getting to the present day. Kathryn sneaks back on stage around puberty, which apparently hit Kyle hard. Sharon doesn't acknowledge Kathryn's return, but that's fine. Kathryn brought cake.

Carl goes on. He talks like he has been waiting his entire life to deliver this speech, and maybe he has. It strikes Kathryn now what it must be like to have someone in your life who has been around since your first words, your first haircut. The closest thing Kathryn has is Chris, who's only known Kathryn since she became this version of herself.

Kathryn's toast is a smash. She sticks closely to the early material, all the hits—Sharon and Kathryn meeting each other on the first day of grad school only to discover that the first day of grad school was actually tomorrow; and then Sharon and Kathryn missing the first day of grad school because they had stayed up all night talking about how excited they were about grad school. It's a good story, even if it's not entirely true.

Kathryn also tells the mostly true story of how Sharon and Kyle fell in love, in which Kathryn played a key role. Kathryn's role was saying, What about Kyle?, over and over for months until Sharon noticed Kyle. What about Kyle, What about Kyle, What about Kyle, Kathryn intones into the microphone. Kyle gives Kathryn a thumbs-up, and this gets a big laugh.

There are other toasts Kathryn could give—toasts that would sound loving and affection-filled to anyone listening, while driving long needles into Sharon's organs. Kathryn has already given those toasts to Chris and Moss and Emily. All the way here, Kathryn gave those toasts and then shot them into the fiery heart of the sun.

That was Emily's idea. Every time Kathryn would finish a venomous toast, Emily would roll down the window and say, That was perfect. Now shoot it into the fiery heart of the sun.

So in the end, all that's left for Kathryn to do is raise her glass and say: To best friends.

Which is a good way to leave it, even if it's not entirely true.

———

Sharon hugs Kathryn there on the stage, is photographed hugging her. Kathryn will never see this photo, but it is lovely. The wedding photographer will use it in his portfolio for years, long after the hairstyles become noticeably dated. He'll always be trying to take another photo like it.

Sharon will see the photo once in a while, usually on anniversaries, and also when her daughter comes home engaged. And every time Sharon sees it, she will feel fonder and warmer toward Kathryn, and will wish the best for Kathryn, wherever she might be. And where *is* she? That's the part Kathryn can't see.

The plan all week was to flee as soon as the toasts were done. Have the engine running, Kathryn had said more than once on the ride up. The promise of it kept her going all day.

Now, though, Kathryn feels liberated, like a country freed of occupiers, and she wants to drink, and dance to popular music.

Of course, Moss does not dance. Chris either, but Kathryn knew that.

I will always dance with you, Emily says.

And it's fun. They dance plainly and unironically. They take off their shoes. They request songs and sometimes sing along. Kathryn feels capable of great things.

Chris and Moss watch them dance from the table. Kathryn glances over frequently to where they are sitting, just to see. Occasionally their lips move, but mostly not. What Kathryn wants is to look over and see the two of them laughing together or talking deeply about some unknown thing they both care about. That's how Kathryn would like to remember this moment. She would really like to remember it that way.

MARCH

CHAPTER 19

What Everybody Wants

WHAT CHRIS WANTS

What Chris wants sometimes is to be at home and just be there. What Chris wants is a good blizzard weekend. A blizzard weekend is when you stop by the grocery store on your way home from work on a Friday and stock up on everything you might need, and then you don't leave the house until you have to go to work on Monday morning. You can do it any weekend; there doesn't need to be a blizzard.

The great thing about a blizzard weekend is there's all this time and space yawning around you. The conversations you have on a blizzard weekend are hand-sewn and delicate. They would never survive the permanent-press cycle of a regular weekend.

The other great thing is that all your books and things are there. So if there's an idea you're trying to surface, some half-glimpsed feeling you're trying to find language for, and you think of an Annie Dillard line that gets at that feeling, you know where the book is on your shelf, you know where the line is on the page, it's right there.

WHAT KATHRYN WANTS

What Kathryn wants is to hang out at Ahimsa. More and more often, Kathryn leaves the apartment to run a quick errand and ends up at Ahimsa making dinner. She calls Chris at work and says he should come, there's pie.

The conversations you have at Ahimsa are sprawling quilts with all hands stitching at once. When you think of an Annie Dillard line, someone says they think Naveed has some Annie Dillard, so you all troop to his room and he says he doesn't think he does, but you can look, so you all tilt your heads to one side and read the spines, and he doesn't have any, but he has some Rumi and there's a line in there that someone loves, and then someone wants to read out the opening paragraphs of *Written on the Body*, and Zachary wants to hear Ickle Me, Pickle Me, Tickle Me Too, and you never do find the Dillard line that gets at that feeling.

WHAT EMILY WANTS

What Emily wants is to live. Living tends to mean live theatre, not film. Living means live music, not lying on the living room floor listening to Bessie Smith records.

Which is not to say that Emily will not lie beside Chris and listen to St. Louis Blues three times in a row and really let it get inside her, the way the trumpet and the vocals wrap themselves around each other, because Emily will do that, her eyes filling up with appreciation. But then she'll want to go do something else.

She'll want to go see her friend Cesar who's got a new band and she'll ask him at the sound check if they know St. Louis Blues and Cesar will say maybe, and later they'll play it as the encore with a musical saw and clarinet and it will be so transcendent that Chris will wish he had a recording of it.

WHAT MOSS WANTS

Chris has no idea what Moss wants.

WHAT CHRIS WANTS

What Chris wants is time alone with Kathryn when they are both awake. He has all these little things to tell her; they're starting to pile up.

Kathryn says why can't he tell her at dinner? Or are these things Chris doesn't want Emily to know about?

It's not that, Chris says. He wants to tell Emily, too. He wants to tell Kathryn and Emily everything. He just wants to tell them individually.

Why is that? Kathryn asks.

Chris doesn't know. It feels different, telling them together.

Kathryn wants to know why the whale story was always sad when Chris told it to Kathryn, and full of wonder when he told it to Emily.

What? Chris says.

Do you see me as a sad person? Kathryn says.

But it's not whales, the things Chris wants to tell her. It's little fluffs, tiny flecks of life, so small and delicate they can only land on one ear at a time.

WHAT KATHRYN WANTS

What Kathryn wants is the four of them together. The four of them cooking elaborate meals together, the four of them standing together under a meteor shower. When any one person is absent, Kathryn gets noticeably less happy.

I just like us, Kathryn says, when Chris presses her on it.

Once, when Moss was out of town on a week-long contract and Emily flew down to see her brother, Kathryn appeared to be dragging herself through the days. It was hard to watch.

Chris tried to love her enough for four.

WHAT EMILY WANTS

What Emily wants is to be Emily. Being Emily means pausing the movie to answer the phone and saying to the person on the other end, Hey you should come over and watch this movie with us, even though you've already started the movie and the person won't understand anything that's happening and you'll have to keep stopping to explain things, because it's Bergman and you can't just drop into a Bergman, but Emily won't mind doing it. And though it ruins the flow and the mood, you'll see things you never saw in the movie, listening to Emily explain it.

Being Emily means bringing home a fragrant backpacker she met on the bus and putting them in the guest room for a month and then when the backpacker leaves, getting postcards from Estonia and Mozambique and Tuscaloosa.

There are a lot of good people, Emily says.

Being Emily means finding the good people and bringing them in.

WHAT MOSS WANTS

Okay, one thing Moss clearly wants is for Kathryn to be happy. When Kathryn puts a silly hat on Moss's head, he leaves it perched there all night. When Kathryn begs to see Moss's supposedly award-winning moonwalk, a childhood secret lodged loose by tequila and tickling, Moss puts Billie Jean on the jukebox and busts a move right there in the bowling alley. Oh yeah, he takes her glo-bowling, which is a sight, the four of them in funny hats, bowling and moonwalking.

For this, Chris is grateful to Moss.

WHAT CHRIS WANTS

What Chris wants, more and more, is to call in sick from life. When he got a sore throat last week, he started right away saying it might be strep, then eased into calling it strep, and said maybe everyone else should stay over at Ahimsa, just to be safe.

He holed up in the apartment for days, said it hurt to talk on the phone. And he did have a sore throat. He wasn't entirely making it up.

WHAT KATHRYN WANTS

What Kathryn wants is to play hooky from work. What Kathryn wants is to say fuck it and go snowshoeing on a Tuesday. What Kathryn wants is to fill a Thermos with mimosas and go to the library and make out.

By Chris's count, Kathryn has turned down the last five contracts she has been offered.

I never wanted to be an indexer, she says.

But what does she want to be? That is what Chris keeps asking.

Sometimes Kathryn tags along when Emily cleans houses, the two of them returning radiant.

I like cleaning houses, Kathryn says. It's rejuvenating.

And she's really good at it, Emily says.

WHAT EMILY WANTS

What Emily wants is for Chris to meet the Other Chris. He's coming to town, the Other Chris is, for a week of shows at some art festival. Emily is already on the guest list, plus one.

It feels important, Emily says simply.

This sways Chris, though he didn't need swaying. Chris will always say yes to Emily.

Which night are we on the list? Chris says.

All the nights. She's on the list for all the nights.

WHAT CHRIS WANTS

What Chris wants is what he had before. He wants to come home after work and make dinner with Kathryn and wash the dishes and hear about her day and tell her about his and watch a little TV and read a chapter in his book and fall asleep. He wants to come home and have nobody say, What should we do tonight?, Where should we do it?, Who should sleep where?

Or he mostly wants that. He wants that maybe six nights a week. And then one night a week he wants to grow as a person.

WHAT KATHRYN WANTS

What Kathryn wants, it's starting to feel like, is to move into Ahimsa.

She asks these questions when they're over there having dinner or hanging out, questions like, How much do you guys pay for rent again? And when they tell her how little it is, Kathryn says, Chris, can you imagine? She appears to be doing some sort of calculation in her head.

She buys work gloves and writes her name on them with black marker and when Ahimsa has work parties she puts them on and goes over.

Chris is waiting for Kathryn's name to appear on their chore chart. He's decided that's when he'll say something.

WHAT CHRIS WANTS

What Chris wants is for Kathryn to be happy. That's what he's always wanted, of course, but now that he's seen what happiness looks like on Kathryn, the sadness of the last nine years terrifies him.

So Chris will do whatever he has to. He will live in that overcrowded house of people. He will learn to tell his stories to two girlfriends at once. And he will wake up in the night to the sound of Kathryn's happiness coming through the walls.

All he wants is for Kathryn to be happy. And Emily, too. And now Moss, he supposes. Chris has nothing against Moss.

APRIL

CHAPTER 20

The Mammoths

Chris is a hard person to break up with.

The first time, Kathryn tried to come at it sideways. They were brushing their teeth. They'd had a nice enough evening, just the two of them for a change, and Kathryn didn't want to come out and say, I think we should break up. So she said, Maybe we should go back to using condoms.

Go back was a misnomer. In reality, Chris and Kathryn had never used condoms. They'd purchased condoms once. They bought a box of twelve together the day they bought everything else for their apartment—towels, plates, salt shaker, toilet brush. It was a big project, starting over with nothing. There was a lot of nesting to do. By the time they got around to needing condoms, it seemed like they might as well go get tested. Kathryn was already on the pill, thanks to Geoffrey. So the twelve condoms had slowly petrified under the bathroom sink.

Yeah, we can do that, Chris burbled from behind his toothbrush. Just like that, he was agreeing to the condom idea, to going back.

But the condoms were not an actual proposal. The condoms were meant to start a conversation about where things stood, and how they'd shifted. The condoms were a signal flare, shot high overhead to illuminate the wreckage and survivors.

There's this thought Kathryn keeps having about space aliens. If space aliens were to come down and look at the evidence, they would conclude that Moss is Kathryn's main person, the one they should abduct along with her.

Certainly if the aliens' objective was breeding humans for some purpose, Moss is the person they would put on board with her. The aliens would simply look at the data.

But even if the aliens measured other things, non-sexual things, if they computed the number of times Kathryn smiled or made jokes, or if they had a machine that measured hope, Moss is still probably the person they'd take.

And the aliens won't care when Kathryn explains that Chris is her life partner and Moss is a guy she's seeing, a great guy, but just a guy. The aliens don't care about nine years together. The aliens will say, We have to go by the evidence. And Kathryn is trying to think of other evidence she might offer, but what?

Does it matter what space aliens think? Emily asks when Kathryn lays out this scenario.

But it does matter. The space aliens want Kathryn to be happy on their planet.

It's not that Moss is better than Chris. No one is better than Chris.

But here's one thing about Moss. Moss plays this game with

Kathryn. Probably Moss doesn't even think of it as a game, but it goes like this: Kathryn will say, What if I went to veterinary school? She'll come out with some random thing like that.

And Moss will say, What if?

So Kathryn says, I'm probably too old. It must be like ten years of school.

And Moss says nothing.

But I was good at science, Kathryn says. She had, after all, taught herself four years of high school science in one summer, and loved doing it.

Moss keeps chopping onions or sanding down some furniture or whatever it is he's doing.

And Kathryn says, I think I could definitely do it.

And then Moss will say—and this is the best part—Moss will say, What then?

And Kathryn gets to describe what her life would be like. She'd love the animals, of course. But she'd get frustrated with their owners, and would frequently complain to friends that the worst thing about her job is that she can't sit down privately with the animal and agree on the best way to proceed, what the animal wants, its concerns and expectations. But Kathryn will be fond of her co-workers, some of whom are younger than her and some older. They will respect and challenge each other and will once a week go out for drinks together at this one place they all like and Kathryn will get very good at darts.

This can go on for hours, Kathryn spinning out the thread and Moss occasionally strumming it with a well-timed what-then.

It all feels so possible. Kathryn can believe in herself as the basically happy, occasionally indignant veterinarian who drinks socially and lives within walking distance of her clinic and has a series of rescued greyhounds named Edith and Gretchen and Tough Guy. That could be her life.

When Kathryn tries playing this game with Chris, they end up on the computer all night looking at course requirements and tuition fees. They research where the best vet schools are and the livability ratings of their respective metropolitan areas.

Chris is unflaggingly supportive. He says, We could definitely make this work, K.

But when Kathryn projects herself into that future, she isn't a different person at all. She's the same miserable person she is now, except surrounded by sick dogs and hissing cats.

We can make it happen, Chris says, and Kathryn tries hard to change the subject.

That's the other good thing about playing with Moss—you can leave off whenever you want. And you don't feel stupid when you wake up the next morning and don't want to go to vet school anymore. You don't even have to say you've decided not to go. You just say, What if I took a graphic design class? What if I got really into beekeeping? And Moss says, What if?

That's how the breaking up started, with a what-if. Kathryn was lolling in bed with Moss and feeling unconscionably happy. She'd been on a roll that night, cracking Moss up with scenarios. What if she became a jewel thief, a flimflam artist, a person of interest. It was dark and fun and then it fell out of her mouth: What if she broke up with Chris.

Hm, Moss said.

Kathryn nudged him with her foot. You're supposed to say, What if.

No, he said, I don't think I am.

Moss was soon asleep, but Kathryn stayed up late with the idea. She was still in love with Chris, she was pretty sure, but did not like herself the way she was with him, so sad and stuck. If only she could break up with herself and leave Chris out of it.

It's better with the four of them together. When Moss and Emily are there, Kathryn can move around inside all the possible versions of herself. She can decide how she wants to respond to stimuli. She is a complex organism.

When she's like this, Kathryn doesn't want to break up with Chris. They work like this. They surprise and delight each other, yet still recognize themselves across the years.

Sometimes Chris will want to head home for the night, just the two of them, and Kathryn will try to carry this complexity home, sloshing around inside her. She always believes she can, but by the time they walk in the door, she's shrunken down to a unicellular spore, thick and tough.

The second time she tries to break up with Chris, Kathryn says, Do you ever feel like we're basically best friends?

Of course, Chris says.

No, Kathryn says, I mean more like friends and less like a couple. A romantic couple. A sexual couple. (The more she says the word *couple*, the less certain she is of anything.)

I suppose, Chris says, yeah.

Kathryn feels a flood of relief and gratitude, to have it out there and agreed upon.

So should we decide that? Kathryn says.

Decide what?

I don't know, make it official.

Like we'd break up?

I'm saying there's nothing *to* break up. We've simply turned into something else.

I'm not breaking up with you, Chris says.

I'm not breaking up either. I'm saying maybe we're not a couple.

I don't think we'd be in the shower together if we were just friends, Chris says.

It goes on like this for days.

Finally a creature crawls out of Kathryn's throat and says this has to stop. The creature pins Chris to the floor, sinks its talons into the carpet, and says, WE LOVE YOU, BUT WE CANNOT BE WITH YOU.

Chris is brave and calm in the face of it. He says he doesn't believe what the creature says, that he doesn't believe in the creature at all.

And the creature says, You're not hearing me.

Chris says all sorts of reasonable things. He is articulate and persuasive. He is impossible not to love.

The creature says, Can you hear me, Chris? Please say you can hear me.

And that's when Chris starts to look scared. When the giant monster that is holding you down starts to beg, it is time to be afraid.

———

They break up on a Friday night and spend the weekend in bed. The first time they have sex, it's to console Chris. The second time, it's Kathryn. After that, it just happens.

Their mouths kiss differently after these months with other people. It takes a while to find what works again, and when they do, Kathryn isn't sure it's the same thing that worked before. Maybe they *can* change; Kathryn doesn't know. In any case, they don't start using condoms now.

Chris doesn't see why they can't still live together.

We could be roommates, he says. Roommates aren't couples.

All the ways that Kathryn tries to explain seem too dire. She talks about tar pits and great mammoths dying slowly in less than a foot of tar.

But the mammoths in that pit, Chris says, they aren't a couple. Pit-mates aren't couples, he says.

Kathryn knows he's teasing, but she also knows that Chris honestly doesn't understand why they can't keep using the same nail clippers and laundry hamper. She wants him to get that. She talks to him about blood clots and prairie fires and standing water.

Chris says, Do the mammoths still love each other? Do the mammoths get to talk on the phone every day?

The big things are surprisingly easy. Chris will keep the bed; Kathryn will take the nightstands. Keep and take are the words they use, and this is how they come to understand that it is Chris who stays and Kathryn who will leave.

I guess you'll go to Ahimsa, Chris says.

I don't know, Kathryn says. We can talk about it.

The smaller things are harder. Patsy, the one oven mitt that doesn't burn your hand. A blanket they watch TV under called Hughie, sometimes Hughie Louie. They've named so many of the objects in their life.

We don't have to figure it all out right now, Kathryn says.

But they can't stop figuring.

What unsettles them both is how many things there are in their home that neither of them wants.

How did they get all this stuff?

It's a tar pit, Chris says. Things collect.

Monday comes. Chris could call in sick, but why? He'd have to go in tomorrow, or the day after that. So he gets up, puts himself in the shower, makes breakfast.

Kathryn follows him around in her pyjamas. Sits on the toilet while he brushes his teeth. Watches him tie his shoes that way he does.

They spend a long time at the front door. Neither of them wants to say goodbye this morning, though they do say it several times. Chris keeps putting his hand on the doorknob, then letting it fall back to his side.

I'll still be here when you get home, Kathryn says.

Right here?

No, Kathryn says.

MAY

JUNE

JULY

AUGUST

SEPTEMBER

CHAPTER 21

Small Craft

6 a.m. is too early to go over. As a rule, Chris tries not to show up at Ahimsa unannounced, though Kathryn has said several times that it's okay. She said at first she wasn't sure how it would be, having Chris over there, but it's been fine. She likes it when he comes over, she says. She always hugs him and sometimes takes his hand, which is interesting.

Still, they said seven, so Chris will kill one more hour. Maybe he can finish another book. He has been rereading all his books and then releasing them into the wild. He left Emma Goldman on a bus. He dropped off a box of Alice Munro at what he thinks is a women's shelter on his way to work. Really, most of these books he was only keeping in case he wanted to read them again someday. So why not read them now and get it over with.

Chris Deming getting rid of books, Kathryn said when she was over last. Should I be worried? she said. She placed her hand inside the empty space of a shelf, like it was a magician's trick.

But it's not like Chris is planning to jump off a bridge. He doesn't know what he'll do when all the books are gone. Maybe he'll buy new books.

6:21. The clock is oppressing him. Chris thinks that if he walked his bike instead of rode, and if he walked slow, and if he stopped a couple times along the way, he could leave right now. He has been up and ready for hours. Has unloaded and reloaded his bike twice. Masturbated. He doesn't know what to do with himself.

Chris has been doing this thing of going to bed earlier and earlier. Sometimes he comes home from work and gets straight under the covers. He wakes up at two or three in the morning and figures he might as well get up and get on with it.

You might be depressed, Kathryn said after this had been going on for a while.

You might be depressed, Chris said, and Kathryn laughed.

They say things like this to each other now, things they would not have said before. Not unkind things, never unkind, but lancing. It makes people nervous. Twice now, Chris and Kathryn have found themselves alone in the Ahimsa kitchen, Emily and Moss and the other housemates having slunk away. But it feels vital, grappling like this. It feels like they are getting at something.

Still, Chris doesn't think he's depressed. He thinks he's a morning person. Sometimes, when he wakes up at two in the morning, he goes and meets up with Emily wherever she is, and instead of falling asleep in a corner, he's fun and funny and awake, until it's Emily who crashes. Then Chris walks to work full of energy and does his job exceedingly well. Does that sound like depression?

One time, Kathryn said. Emily told me that happened one time.

Chris dawdles along and manages to arrive at Ahimsa almost five minutes late. No one is ready. Well, Kathryn is ready. Chris spots her bike, tightly packed and leaned against a tree. But Kendra and Naveed are not even outside yet. Miriam is holding a cup of tea and an inner tube. Emily is waiting for someone who should be here any minute to drop off a bike for her. We won't make it as far as the first ferry, Chris thinks.

Moss, by his truck, nods once to Chris. The nod means: I admire your locomotion and the competence with which you have prepared your gear.

Chris knows from talking to Kathryn that Moss is embarrassed about taking the truck, that Moss has strong ideas about what is and what isn't camping. But bringing the truck was the only way to get everyone to come, and now it is filled with lawn chairs and god knows what. People keep loading more in.

They finally roll out around eight thirty, the mess of them strung out in a line. It's Kathryn first, then Naveed+Zachary, Miriam, Yvonne the girlfriend, Emily, and last, Chris. Kendra is in the truck with Moss.

Chris can hear Emily's chain grinding and slipping. He can hear the grumble of traffic, already busier than he'd like. He can hear Zachary singing Yellow Submarine, just the chorus, over and over. Chris might be able to do something about the chain, he thinks. He'll take a look at the next rest stop.

The sun has burned off the morning. The uphills stretch out for miles.

Chris keeps seeing the ugly blue tent on the back of Kathryn's bike and thinking, Hey, *there's* my tent. But Chris has a new tent now. It's red and supposedly better.

Chris had wanted to buy the same tent he had before—he got Kathryn to read him the model number over the phone— but apparently they don't make that one anymore. The sales- person showed Chris the replacement model, and all the ways they had improved it. She seemed very keen, the salesperson. She climbed into the floor model with Chris and zipped up the hatch. They lay side by side, so he could get a feel for it with two people. It's possible she was flirting with him. Chris just wanted to know if it came in any kind of blue.

They make slow progress, but everyone seems in good cheer. Chris decides to leave the chain alone, decides not to hear it. It doesn't appear to be bothering Emily, who keeps turning around and smiling at Chris, encouragingly, like he's the one who might be struggling.

Still here, he says.

Chris wonders if Emily will end up sleeping in his new tent with him, or if he will sleep in her borrowed one, or neither. They haven't talked about it, but that doesn't necessarily mean anything. Things have been a little strange with Emily since the breakup, and Chris is trying not to make them stranger.

What he can't figure out is why he and Emily spend only two or three nights a week together. Yes, it's more than before the breakup, but what's strange to Chris is why not every night?

On the big ferry, they all go upstairs and eat lemon meringue pie. They take turns in a vibrating chair. They roam in a pack like a loud, happy family or bike gang. Chris spends five dollars introducing Zachary to Ms. Pac-Man. I like the part where I get to chase the ghosts, Zachary says. I don't like the part where the ghosts chase me.

Later, on the small ferry, Chris breaks down and looks at Emily's chain. Emily is over talking to some tourists from Australia. It's fairly easy to fix the grinding. The slipping is a bigger problem. He'd have to break open the chain, pry off a link or two, reconnect the ends. If it was Kathryn's bike, if it was Kathryn's bike six months ago, his fingers would already be in there. But he isn't sure that's how he's supposed to be with Emily. In any case, the grinding is gone.

Chris goes over to stand with Kathryn and Moss, because they are not, at the moment, hugging. Moss nods. This nod means: I welcome your presence. You are no enemy here.

Chris kind of likes Moss. Last month, Chris finished rereading Gabriel García Márquez and brought the whole stack to Moss. They had a moment, there in the kitchen. Moss went upstairs and came back with a worn paperback, *The Hour of the Star*, and put it in Chris's hand. Chris tried to explain he was in de-acquisition mode, but in the end he took the book. They haven't spoken about it since, not out loud, but Chris feels they have an understanding.

It occurs to Chris now that instead of trying so hard to convince Emily to move in with him, Chris should've asked Moss. They could circle around the apartment in companionable silence, like goldfish.

Emily didn't want to move in. Chris really wanted it. It made so much sense to Chris. They both slept better the nights they spent at his place. They could eat whenever and whatever they wanted. They could take a bath without someone asking through the door how much longer they'd be. The first time Emily had come and spent the whole weekend at his place, she'd lain naked in a sunbeam moving across the living room floor and said she wished this weekend would never end. So why not move in? At the very least, it seemed like something they should consider. But Emily said, I don't think we're those people, Chris.

Chris is still trying to figure out what people they are.

You're making her too mysterious, Kathryn said. Why do you do that? I know that's not all she told you.

It's true. Emily also said that moving in with him wouldn't be good for either of them. She said that she loves staying over at his apartment once in a while, having the whole place to themselves, the stillness and calm of it, the walking around in their underwear; but that day to day she wouldn't thrive living with just one person, no matter how much she adored that one person. She said she needs the cross-pollination of bumping up against a bunch of people every day. She said she'd be thrilled for Chris to move into Ahimsa someday if Kathryn was comfortable with it, but that she, Emily, isn't sure that's what Chris needs. She said Chris might need something different, and it could take them a while to work out what that was. She said, no, she wasn't breaking up with him. She said she loves him and that they should keep doing what they were doing and see what happens.

So they're seeing what happens.

They must be halfway across when the motor on the small ferry stops. A sudden silence rises up and washes over the deck. Everyone looks at the person beside them and says, with their eyes or their lips, What's going on?

The ferry slows and slows and slows to a dead drift.

The idea of whales spreads through the crowd and soon everybody is at the railing squinting out at the possibility. Children run from starboard to port and back, because no one knows where to look. Video cameras film full minutes of unbreached ocean.

You hear some people start to complain, as if the whales are a rock band who are taking too long to get on stage. Chris would like to say this to Kathryn, later, when they retell this story.

Then the motor rumbles up again and the ferry turns around in a wide arc and heads back in the direction they came from. Now a different idea jolts through the crowd. The word you hear people whispering is bomb.

Chris estimates there are 150 people on board. He isn't sure why a body count is his first instinct, but having a number feels important. There isn't much else to do. Just stand in a clump with the people you know and see what happens.

The motor cuts out after only a minute and they drift again in silence.

––––––

The captain comes out of the loudspeaker. He says you might have noticed we've had a change of course. He says that a member of the crew spotted some gear in the water and that they've circled back to check on the situation, make sure no one is in need of assistance.

Now everyone is back at the railing, looking out for anything, they don't know what: a life jacket, a bobbing head, a waving arm, a first aid kit, a flashlight. No one is complaining anymore.

After some minutes, there is shouting near the bow, and pointing, and then they all see it, a glimpse of safety orange disappearing and reappearing in the chop. The ferry creeps forward and people call out, We're coming. Hold on.

When they are closer, though, they can see it is only a paddle. Orange and collapsible. Two crew members fish it out of the water and hurry away with it.

We should spread out, someone says. And people do. Birders fetch binoculars from their cars and pass them around. Someone spots a bottle of Dr Pepper in the water, and later a blue flip-flop.

The ferry makes a slow circle, but mostly the motor is kept silent. Every few minutes, the ship's horn lets out a long, sober blast, and then everyone listens together. It's the only time they take their eyes off the water, to listen.

After an hour or so, the Coast Guard arrives with boats and a helicopter. The ferry is sent on its way, though some believe they should stay and help. The captain thanks everyone for their patience and apologizes for the delay. It was probably nothing, the captain says. It's usually nothing, but you've got to make sure. That water's mighty cold.

———

Kathryn has booked four campsites, all in a cluster on the far edge of the park. The sites are a long way from everything—the bathrooms, the water spigot—but they're secluded. The only people you see when you look around are the people you came with. Chris likes that.

The tents go up easily. There are more than enough hands. Moss and Kathryn have signed up to cook the first night, so there's nothing much to do.

Zachary takes Chris out exploring. They find a rocky little cove nearby, too barnacled and kelpy to attract people from the good side of the park. This too, Chris likes.

Chris sits on a large bleached-out log and watches Zachary try to skip stones in the water.

I almost did it that time, Zachary says every time.

After dinner, there's a fire to stare at. Stories come loose. Chocolate is passed around. Chris sits in the circle as long as he can, waiting for someone to make a move toward bed. He figures once one person stands and yawns and says they'd better be turning in, it will put something in motion. And Chris wants to be there when Emily starts thinking about bed. He doesn't want to rush her—not that Emily can be rushed—but he does want to make himself available. He likes sleeping with her. He likes the way she falls asleep with her hand scrunching and unscrunching his shirt. He likes her breath in the morning. He likes hearing the first words out of her mouth.

After a while, though, Chris slips away from the fire and zips himself into his tent. He can still hear them talking long after he's asleep.

———

It must be three or four in the morning when Chris wakes up. His watch has lost its glow. He had thought maybe he would roll over in the night and find Emily curled alongside him, but no, Emily, it seems, is in her own tent, a few feet away.

Maybe tomorrow night. It is a long weekend, after all.

It's lonely in the tent. He's lonely a lot of the time, Chris finds. For the first few months, he wasn't sure what that feeling was. He didn't recognize it. It wasn't until Miriam said, You must get lonely over there, that Chris realized, Oh.

Kathryn keeps saying Chris should date. She never says who, exactly, just that there are people out there. You shouldn't expect one person to be your everything. Kathryn and Moss have separate bedrooms and sleep resolutely apart one night a week, so Kathryn gets to say things like this now.

This idea that he would date horrifies Chris. It's like Kathryn has forgotten who he is.

I want the opposite of dating, Chris says. I want someone to stay home with on a Friday night and play Scrabble in our pyjamas. I want to make a giant pot of soup together and then fall asleep with my head in their lap while they read, or their head in my lap.

You had that, Kathryn says. And you wanted something else.

Outside, birds start calling to each other. Chris unzips his tent as slowly and quietly as he can and stands up into the pre-dawn air. He looks around for clues about how late everyone else stayed up. Sometimes you can tell from the number of empties scattered around on the ground, or the food forgotten and left out.

But everything is tidy and stowed away. The fire is properly extinguished. These are good campers, you have to admit.

Chris makes his way down to the water and watches the sky fade in. He had hoped there would be a sunrise. He liked the thought of telling Emily he got up and saw a spectacular sunrise, and Emily wanting to wake up with him tomorrow to come see. Instead the sun sneaks up somewhere else, probably on the good side of the park. They can have it, Chris thinks.

Soon, Zachary comes bounding down the trail full of stories. He heard an owl in the night. He got to pee outside and his dad peed, too. He saw stars, stars, stars.

Is anyone else up? Chris asks.

They're being boring, Zachary says.

Chris knows that Emily won't wake up for hours. Maybe he will make her coffee and bring it to her tent and kiss her blinking eyes. Maybe he will let her sleep. He has so much love coiling around inside him.

The thing that bothers Chris about Kathryn's whole you-should-date idea is the insinuation that he could just pick someone. It took Chris twenty-some years to find Kathryn; nine more to find Emily. Who knows how long it'll be before Chris meets another person who cracks him open like that.

And until then he's supposed to what? Date? Chris doesn't want to kill time with the cute, friendly woman who sells tents, as appealing as she might be.

He wants to get ready. Ready for what, he doesn't know. But for starters, he wants to not have all those old books filling his shelves. He wants to not have boxes in the hall closet that say MISC. He wants to use up that 500g bag of caraway seeds that has been in the kitchen cabinet forever. He has started taking one seed a day and carrying it around in his mouth.

Watch, watch, Zachary says. This one is perfect.

He holds up a small, flat stone for Chris to see, and then turns and hurls it at the water. It disappears with a plunk.

I almost-almost did it, Zachary says.

You're getting there, Chris says, though he can see the poor kid might be years from getting there. Chris tries to think of what helpful advice he could offer. He does know how to skip stones, after all, but he can't remember learning the trick to it. All he can remember is that he couldn't do it, he couldn't do it, he couldn't do it, and then he could.

ACKNOWLEDGEMENTS

Early versions of the opening chapters appeared in *The Malahat Review* and *The New Quarterly*. Thanks to John Barton, Kim Jernigan, and everyone at these crucial and subscription-worthy publications. Thanks to John Metcalf and the folks at Oberon Press for giving those stories a second life in *Best Canadian Stories*. And thanks to Anita Chong, McClelland & Stewart, and everyone involved in the Journey Prize for including "Sleep World" in the anthology, which felt to me like winning.

This book wouldn't be a book if it weren't for Martha Webb, indefatigable and known for her miracles. Heartfelt thanks to her and everyone at the McDermid Agency. I am also profoundly grateful to my editors, Kiara Kent and Liese Mayer, who believed in the book and made it immeasurably better with the lightest touch. I cannot imagine a better pair of champions.

I'm thankful to the wonderful writers—Clea Young, Doretta Lau, Théodora Armstrong, Susan Mersereau, Anna Ling Kaye, Lila Yomtoob, Susan Sanford Blades, Anna Swanson, Kevin

Chong—who filled my margins with questions and insights and exhortations. And to the noble souls who read early drafts as they dribbled out and gave me a reason to keep going. Thank you Nikki Scott, Kirby Huminuik, Keshav Mukunda, Louise Tremblay, Sharon Eisman, and Ken Tsui.

Huge thanks to Hal Wake and the Vancouver Writers Fest. To Jaki, who first channelled the Tuna Voice. To Mrs. Riley, who was exactly the teacher I needed. To Jan and Kirby, who made me family. And to my parents, who are still in love and showed me what it looks like.

Finally, love and eternal gratitude to Pam and Rachel who saved my life for all those years, and Susannah who gave it back to me.

ABOUT THE AUTHOR

ZOEY LEIGH PETERSON was born in England, grew up all over the United States, and now lives in Canada. Her fiction has appeared in *The Walrus, EVENT, Grain, PRISM international,* and has been anthologized in *The Journey Prize Stories* and *Best Canadian Stories*. She is the recipient of the Far Horizons Award for Short Fiction (*The Malahat Review*) and the Peter Hinchcliffe Fiction Award (*The New Quarterly*). *Next Year, For Sure* is her first novel.

A NOTE ABOUT THE TYPE

Next Year, For Sure is set in Monotype Van Dijck, a face originally designed by Christoffel van Dijck, a Dutch typefounder (and sometimes goldsmith) of the seventeenth century. While the roman font may not have been cut by van Dijck himself, the italic, for which original punches survive, is almost certainly his work. The face first made its appearance circa 1606. It was re-cut for modern use in 1937.